Resilience Birthright

Origins of Resilience

Jessica Jane Robinson

Limited Edition
2018

Illustrated by
Charlo Nocete

The Saga of

Resilience Birthright

Origins of Resilience

By Jessica Jane Robinson

THIS IS A RESILIENCE BIRTHRIGHT BOOK
PUBLISHED BY RESILIENCE BIRTHRIGHT, LLC
www.resiliencebirthright.com

ISBN 978-0-9997226-0-2
Written by
Jessica Jane Robinson
Storyboard by
Jessica Jane Robinson

Illustrated and Color by
Charlo Nocete

Printed in PRC

Special Thanks…

I would like to thank my team for their support and help along the way. Juanita Blair, Jennifer Abbe, and Ruth Abbe for helping proof read my script. Charlo Nocete, Grisel Loyola Lopez, and Kenny Estrella for working with me and translating my rough draft storyboards into my vision.

I would also like to thank all those dear and true to my heart who encouraged me to keep going and manifest my dreams. They say it takes a village to raise a child, and I am releasing this graphic novel because so many have loved me enough to help see me through.

Please Note:
This chapter is set on the planet of Terravitae. Therefore, all wording is a rough translation of the Evolusarian language.

Dear Zevi

I hope you enjoy the first story of the zero waste superhero, Resilience. We all have the power to heal the planet. Together we can restore Mother Earth!

Jessica Jane

aka: Resilience

XO

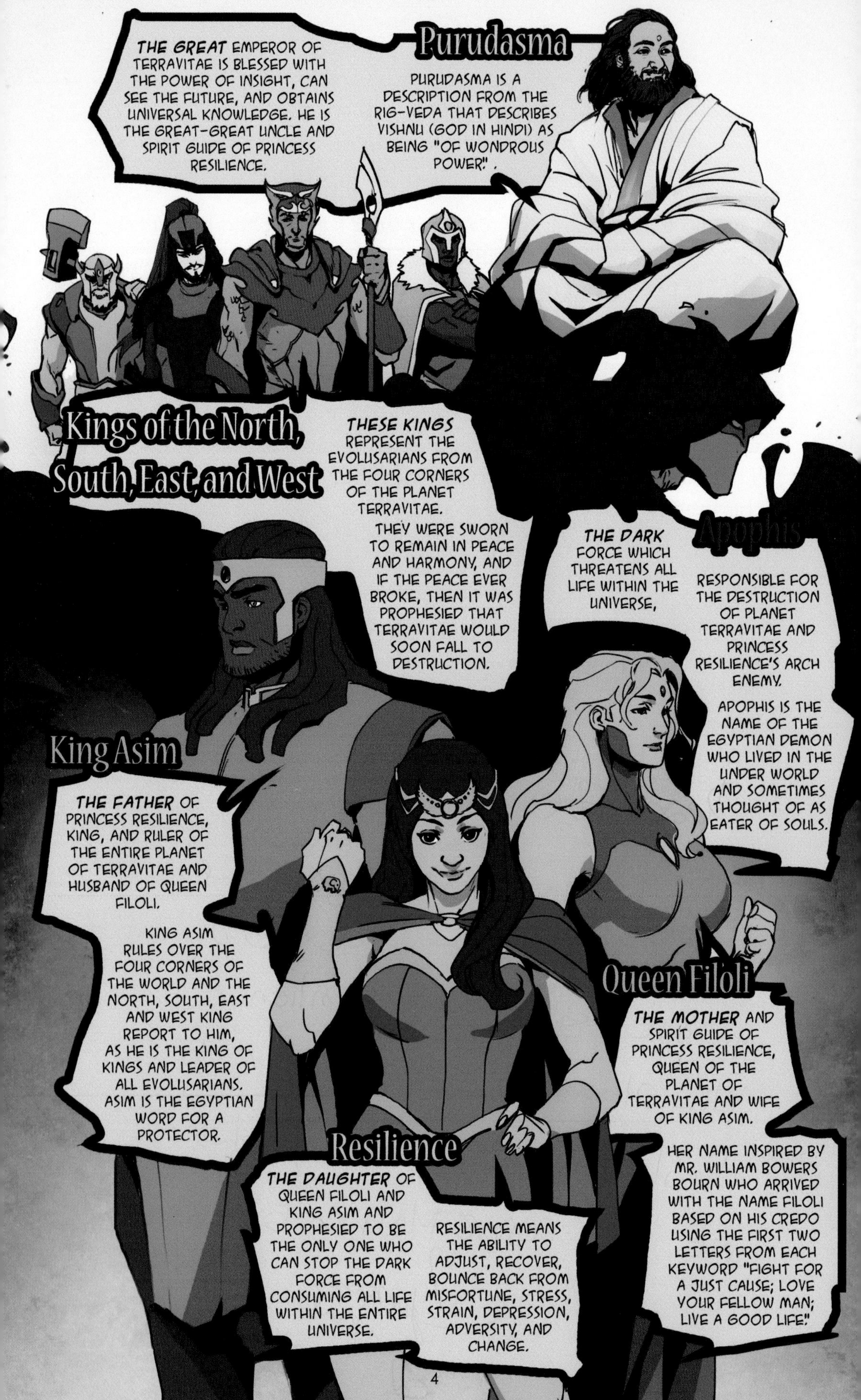
Purudasma
THE GREAT EMPEROR OF TERRAVITAE IS BLESSED WITH THE POWER OF INSIGHT, CAN SEE THE FUTURE, AND OBTAINS UNIVERSAL KNOWLEDGE. HE IS THE GREAT-GREAT UNCLE AND SPIRIT GUIDE OF PRINCESS RESILIENCE.
PURUDASMA IS A DESCRIPTION FROM THE RIG-VEDA THAT DESCRIBES VISHNU (GOD IN HINDI) AS BEING "OF WONDROUS POWER".
Kings of the North, South, East, and West
THESE KINGS REPRESENT THE EVOLUSARIANS FROM THE FOUR CORNERS OF THE PLANET TERRAVITAE.
THEY WERE SWORN TO REMAIN IN PEACE AND HARMONY, AND IF THE PEACE EVER BROKE, THEN IT WAS PROPHESIED THAT TERRAVITAE WOULD SOON FALL TO DESTRUCTION.
Apophis
THE DARK FORCE WHICH THREATENS ALL LIFE WITHIN THE UNIVERSE,
RESPONSIBLE FOR THE DESTRUCTION OF PLANET TERRAVITAE AND PRINCESS RESILIENCE'S ARCH ENEMY.
APOPHIS IS THE NAME OF THE EGYPTIAN DEMON WHO LIVED IN THE UNDER WORLD AND SOMETIMES THOUGHT OF AS EATER OF SOULS.
King Asim
THE FATHER OF PRINCESS RESILIENCE, KING, AND RULER OF THE ENTIRE PLANET OF TERRAVITAE AND HUSBAND OF QUEEN FILOLI.
KING ASIM RULES OVER THE FOUR CORNERS OF THE WORLD AND THE NORTH, SOUTH, EAST AND WEST KING REPORT TO HIM, AS HE IS THE KING OF KINGS AND LEADER OF ALL EVOLUSARIANS. ASIM IS THE EGYPTIAN WORD FOR A PROTECTOR.
Queen Filoli
THE MOTHER AND SPIRIT GUIDE OF PRINCESS RESILIENCE, QUEEN OF THE PLANET OF TERRAVITAE AND WIFE OF KING ASIM.
HER NAME INSPIRED BY MR. WILLIAM BOWERS BOURN WHO ARRIVED WITH THE NAME FILOLI BASED ON HIS CREDO USING THE FIRST TWO LETTERS FROM EACH KEYWORD "FIGHT FOR A JUST CAUSE; LOVE YOUR FELLOW MAN; LIVE A GOOD LIFE."
Resilience
THE DAUGHTER OF QUEEN FILOLI AND KING ASIM AND PROPHESIED TO BE THE ONLY ONE WHO CAN STOP THE DARK FORCE FROM CONSUMING ALL LIFE WITHIN THE ENTIRE UNIVERSE.
RESILIENCE MEANS THE ABILITY TO ADJUST, RECOVER, BOUNCE BACK FROM MISFORTUNE, STRESS, STRAIN, DEPRESSION, ADVERSITY, AND CHANGE.

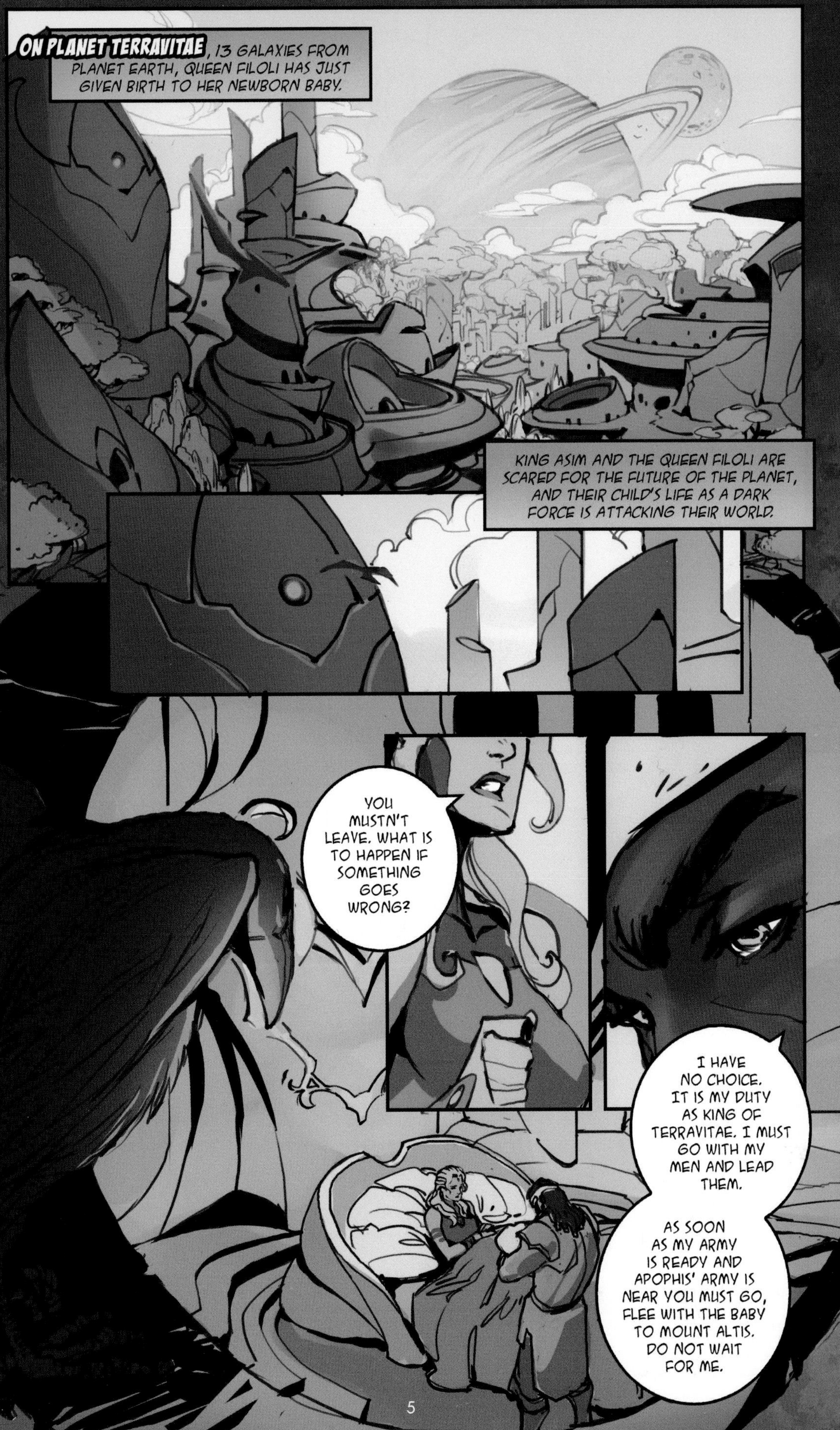
ON PLANET TERRAVITAE, 13 GALAXIES FROM PLANET EARTH, QUEEN FILOLI HAS JUST GIVEN BIRTH TO HER NEWBORN BABY.
KING ASIM AND THE QUEEN FILOLI ARE SCARED FOR THE FUTURE OF THE PLANET, AND THEIR CHILD'S LIFE AS A DARK FORCE IS ATTACKING THEIR WORLD.
YOU MUSTN'T LEAVE. WHAT IS TO HAPPEN IF SOMETHING GOES WRONG?
I HAVE NO CHOICE. IT IS MY DUTY AS KING OF TERRAVITAE. I MUST GO WITH MY MEN AND LEAD THEM.
AS SOON AS MY ARMY IS READY AND APOPHIS' ARMY IS NEAR YOU MUST GO, FLEE WITH THE BABY TO MOUNT ALTIS. DO NOT WAIT FOR ME.

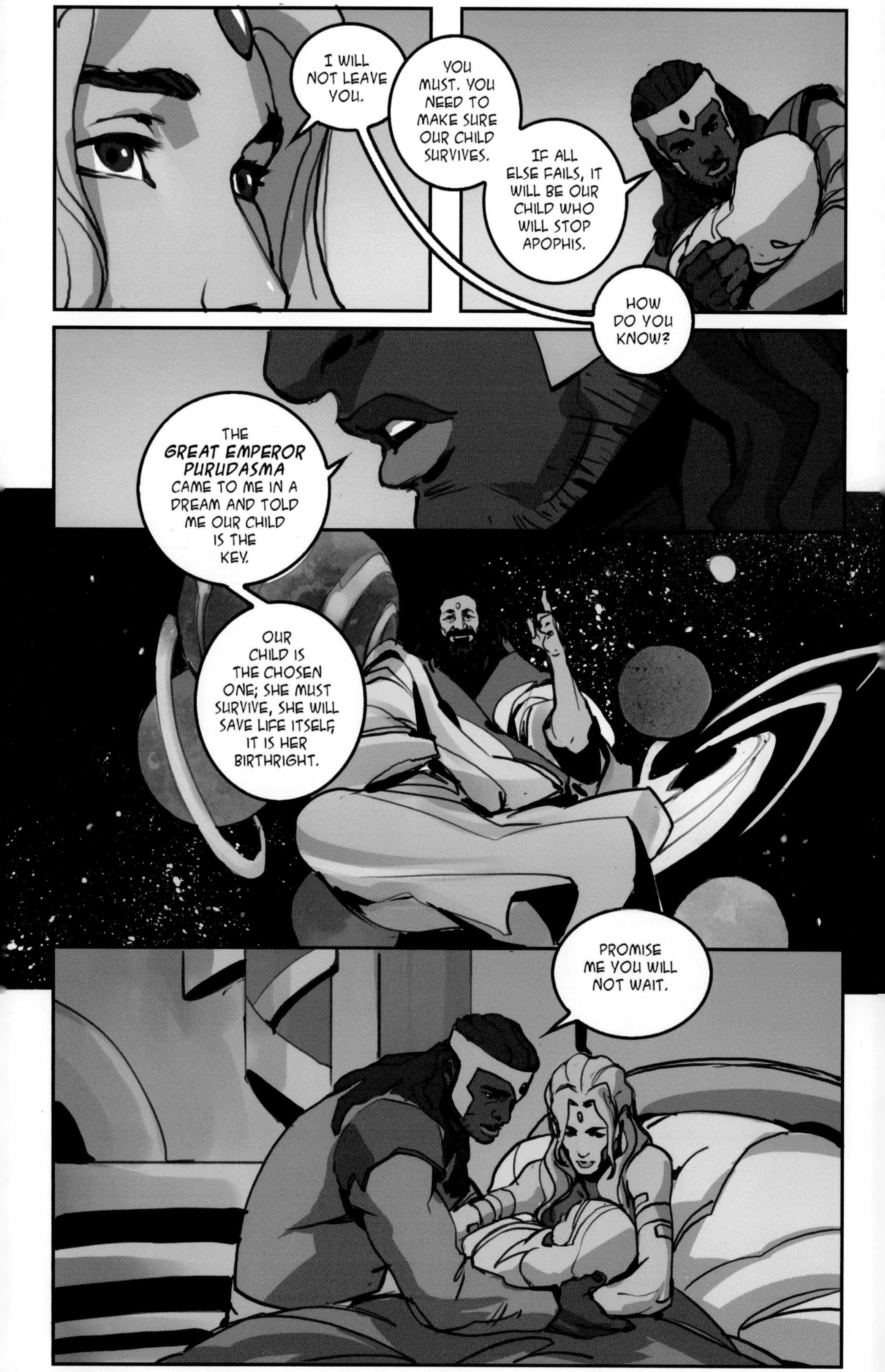
I WILL NOT LEAVE YOU.
YOU MUST. YOU NEED TO MAKE SURE OUR CHILD SURVIVES.
IF ALL ELSE FAILS, IT WILL BE OUR CHILD WHO WILL STOP APOPHIS.
HOW DO YOU KNOW?
THE GREAT EMPEROR PURUDASMA CAME TO ME IN A DREAM AND TOLD ME OUR CHILD IS THE KEY.
OUR CHILD IS THE CHOSEN ONE; SHE MUST SURVIVE, SHE WILL SAVE LIFE ITSELF, IT IS HER BIRTHRIGHT.
PROMISE ME YOU WILL NOT WAIT.

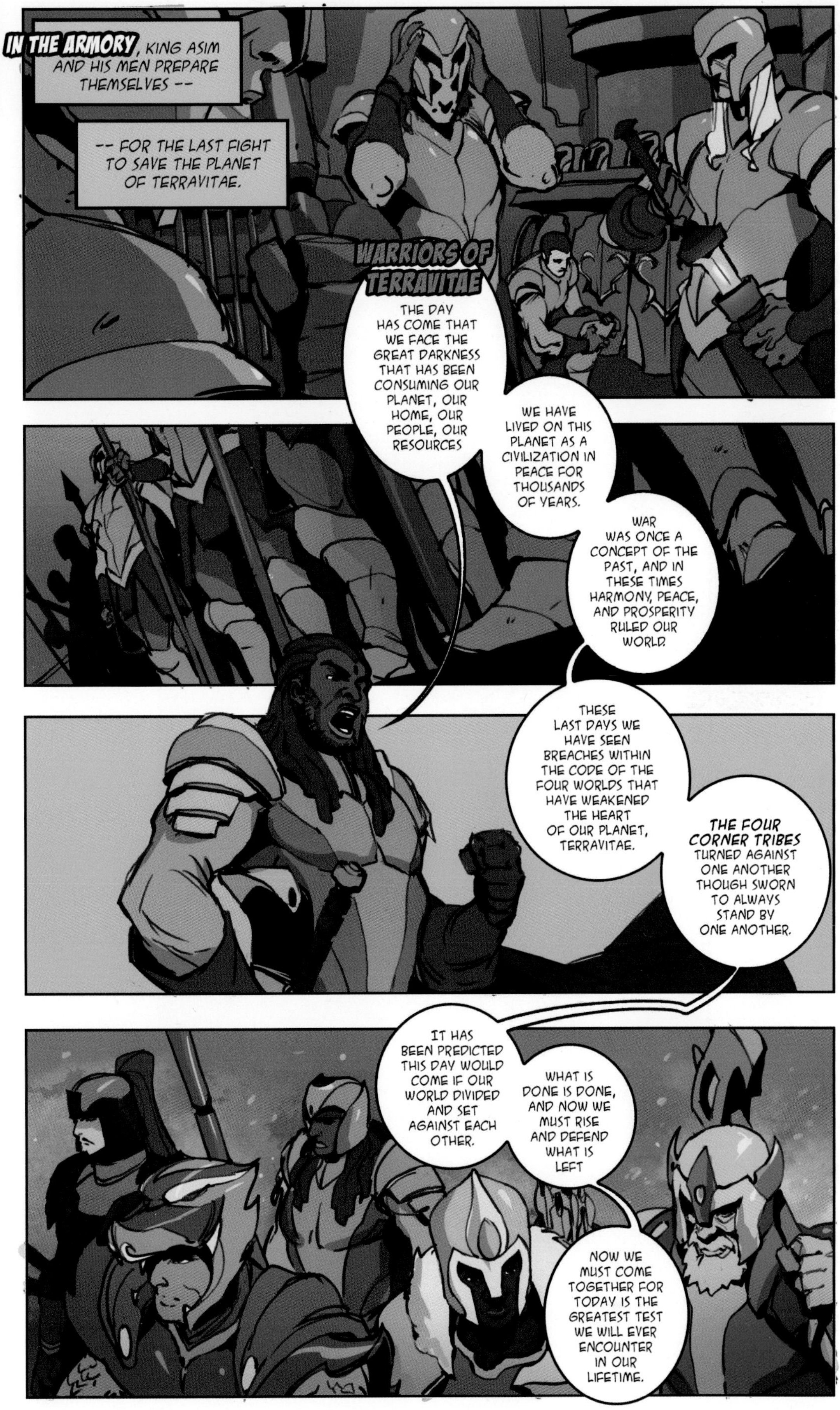
IN THE ARMORY, KING ASIM AND HIS MEN PREPARE THEMSELVES --
-- FOR THE LAST FIGHT TO SAVE THE PLANET OF TERRAVITAE.
WARRIORS OF TERRAVITAE
THE DAY HAS COME THAT WE FACE THE GREAT DARKNESS THAT HAS BEEN CONSUMING OUR PLANET, OUR HOME, OUR PEOPLE, OUR RESOURCES
WE HAVE LIVED ON THIS PLANET AS A CIVILIZATION IN PEACE FOR THOUSANDS OF YEARS.
WAR WAS ONCE A CONCEPT OF THE PAST, AND IN THESE TIMES HARMONY, PEACE, AND PROSPERITY RULED OUR WORLD.
THESE LAST DAYS WE HAVE SEEN BREACHES WITHIN THE CODE OF THE FOUR WORLDS THAT HAVE WEAKENED THE HEART OF OUR PLANET, TERRAVITAE.
THE FOUR CORNER TRIBES TURNED AGAINST ONE ANOTHER THOUGH SWORN TO ALWAYS STAND BY ONE ANOTHER.
IT HAS BEEN PREDICTED THIS DAY WOULD COME IF OUR WORLD DIVIDED AND SET AGAINST EACH OTHER.
WHAT IS DONE IS DONE, AND NOW WE MUST RISE AND DEFEND WHAT IS LEFT
NOW WE MUST COME TOGETHER FOR TODAY IS THE GREATEST TEST WE WILL EVER ENCOUNTER IN OUR LIFETIME.

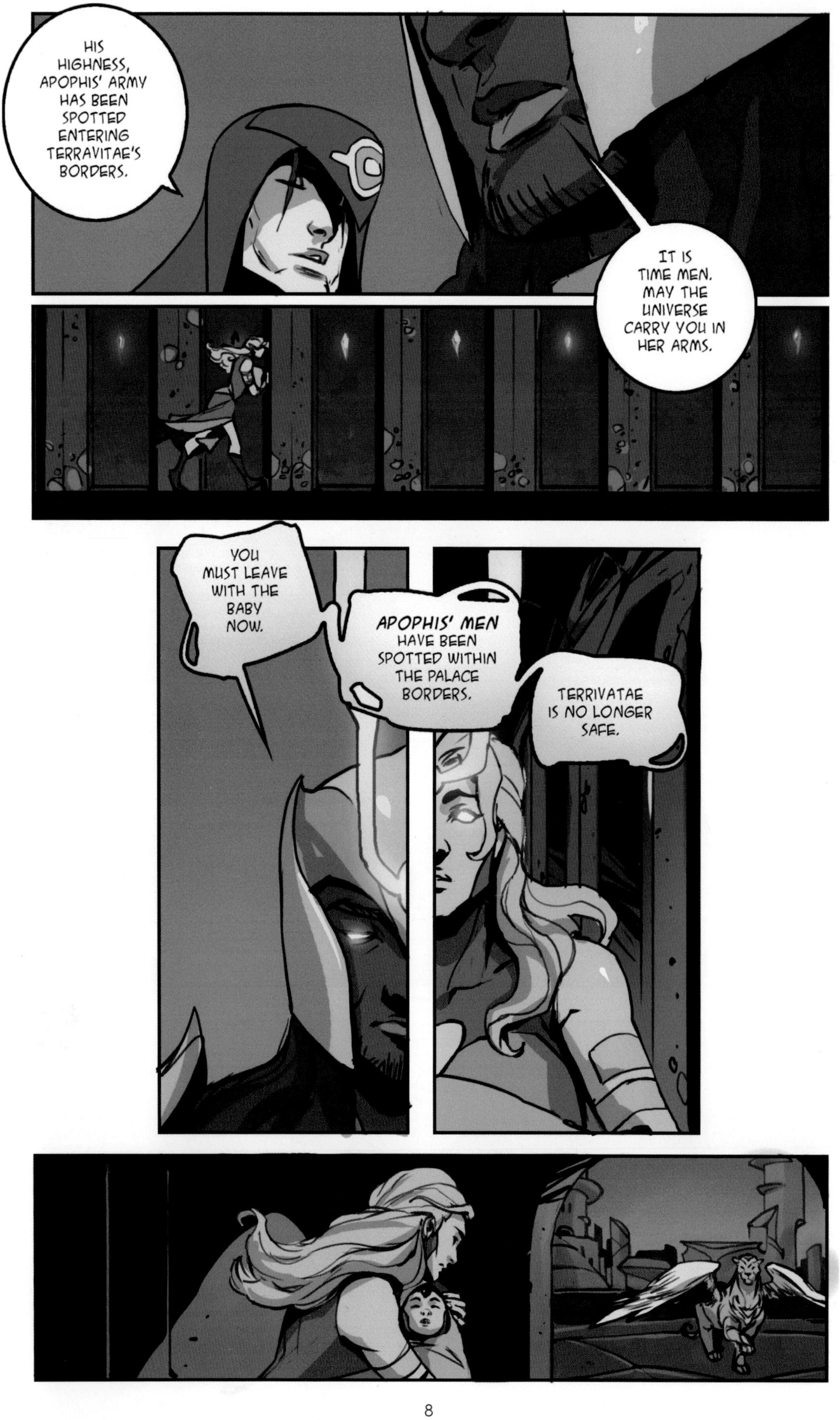
HIS HIGHNESS, APOPHIS' ARMY HAS BEEN SPOTTED ENTERING TERRAVITAE'S BORDERS.
IT IS TIME MEN. MAY THE UNIVERSE CARRY YOU IN HER ARMS.
YOU MUST LEAVE WITH THE BABY NOW.
APOPHIS' MEN HAVE BEEN SPOTTED WITHIN THE PALACE BORDERS.
TERRIVATAE IS NO LONGER SAFE.

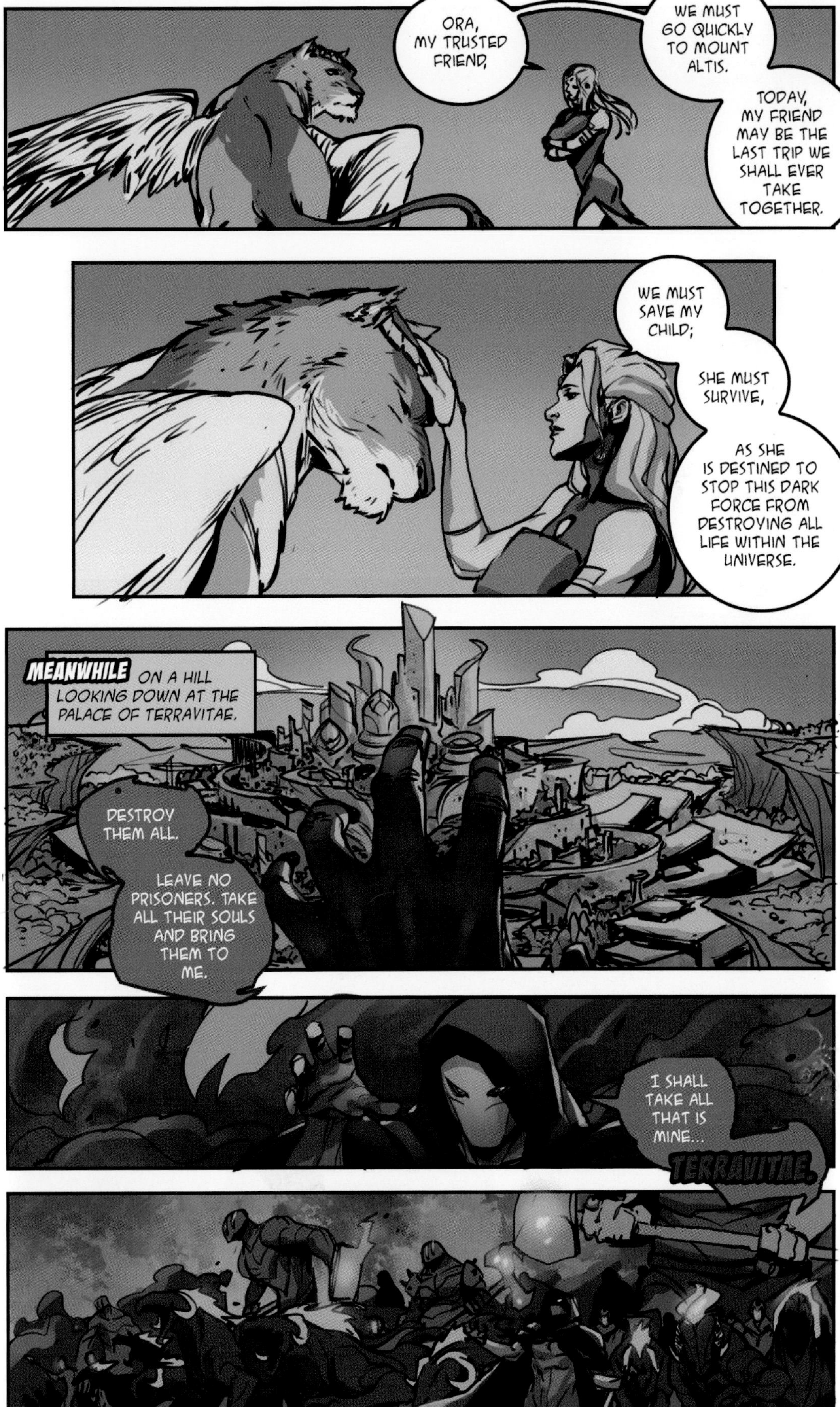
ORA, MY TRUSTED FRIEND,
WE MUST GO QUICKLY TO MOUNT ALTIS.
TODAY, MY FRIEND MAY BE THE LAST TRIP WE SHALL EVER TAKE TOGETHER.
WE MUST SAVE MY CHILD;
SHE MUST SURVIVE,
AS SHE IS DESTINED TO STOP THIS DARK FORCE FROM DESTROYING ALL LIFE WITHIN THE UNIVERSE.
MEANWHILE ON A HILL LOOKING DOWN AT THE PALACE OF TERRAVITAE.
DESTROY THEM ALL.
LEAVE NO PRISONERS. TAKE ALL THEIR SOULS AND BRING THEM TO ME.
I SHALL TAKE ALL THAT IS MINE...
TERRAVITAE.

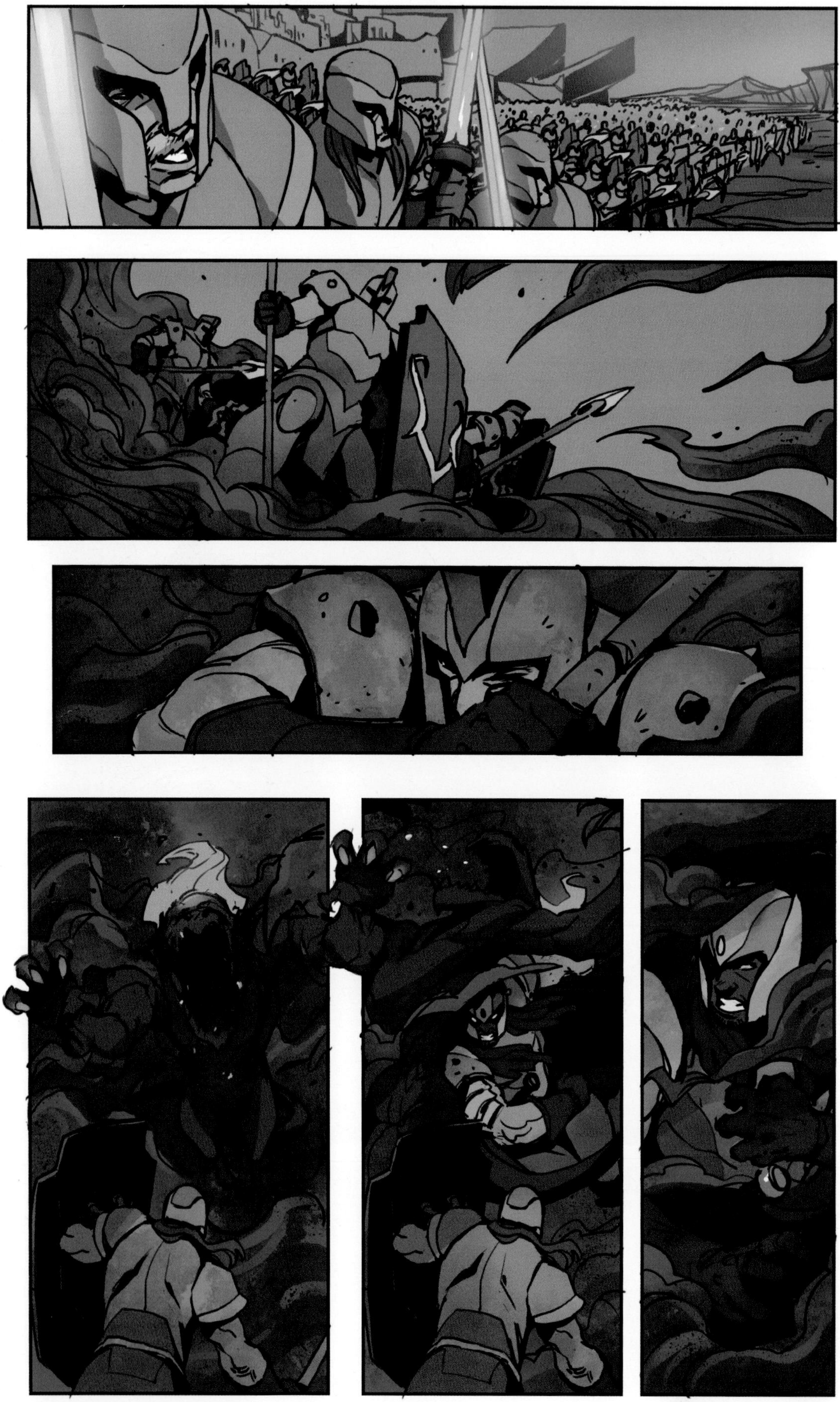

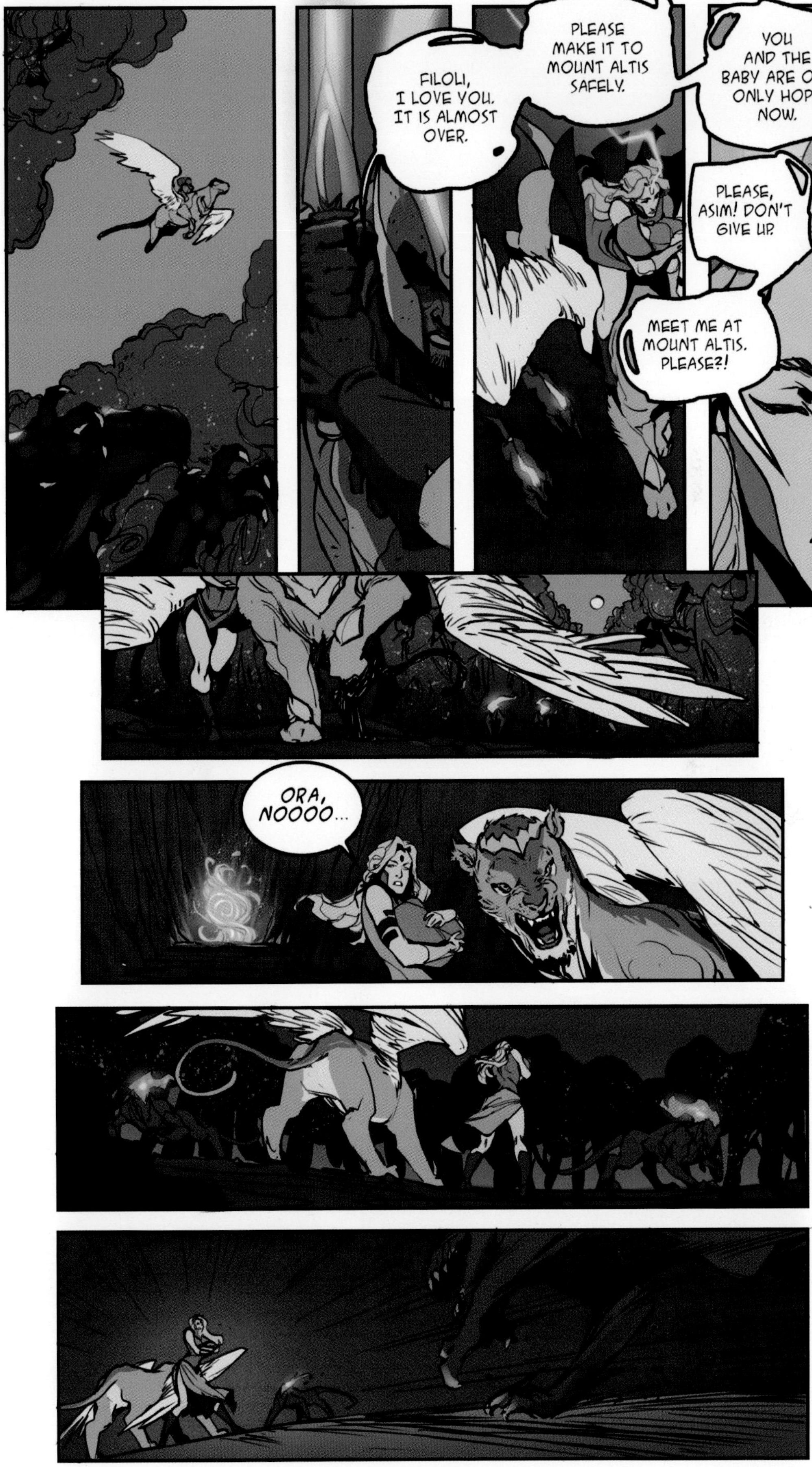
FILOLI, I LOVE YOU. IT IS ALMOST OVER.
PLEASE MAKE IT TO MOUNT ALTIS SAFELY.
YOU AND THE BABY ARE OUR ONLY HOPE NOW.
PLEASE, ASIM! DON'T GIVE UP.
MEET ME AT MOUNT ALTIS. PLEASE?!
ORA, NOOOO...

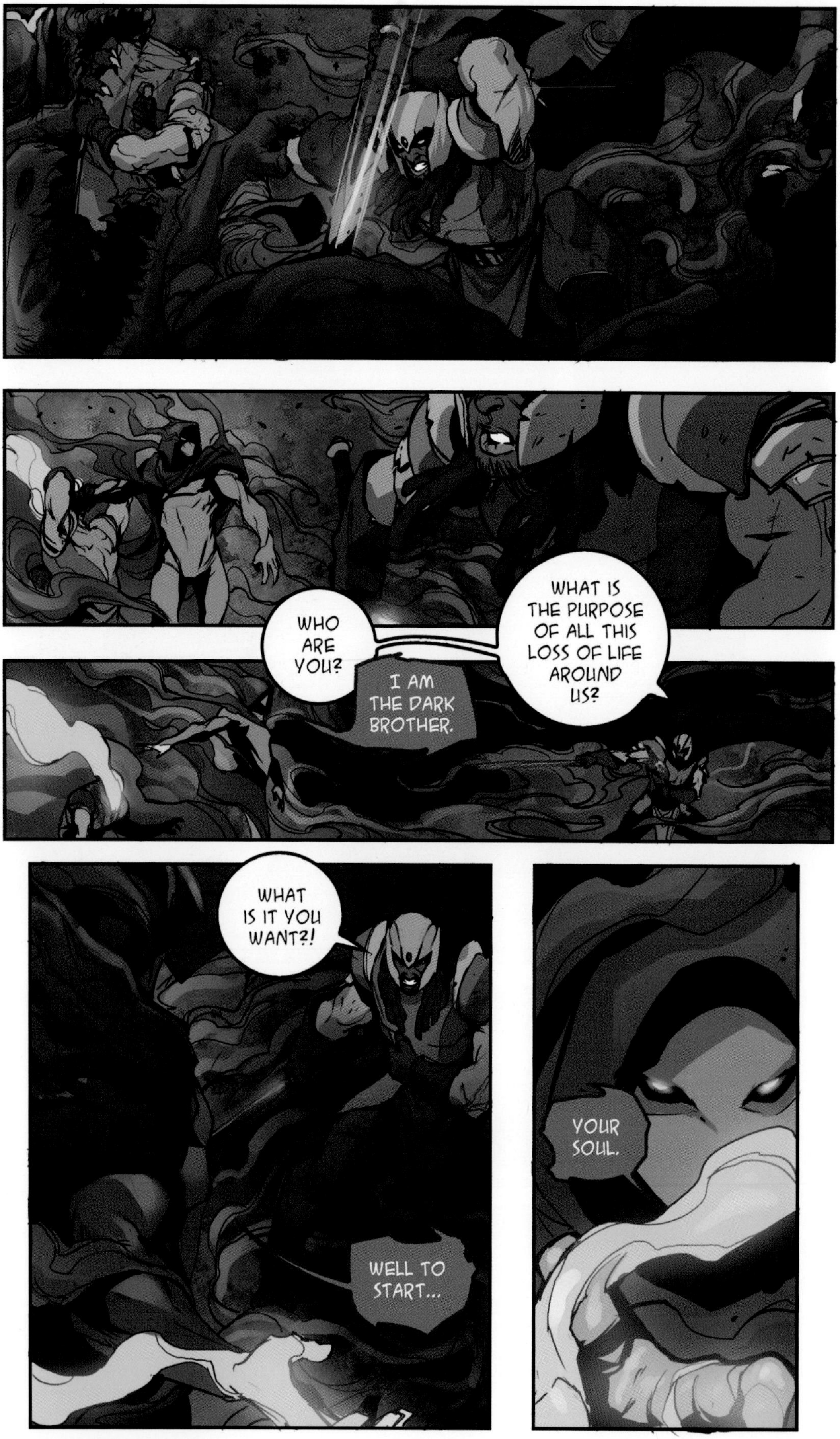
WHO ARE YOU?
WHAT IS THE PURPOSE OF ALL THIS LOSS OF LIFE AROUND US?
I AM THE DARK BROTHER.
WHAT IS IT YOU WANT?!
WELL TO START...
YOUR SOUL.

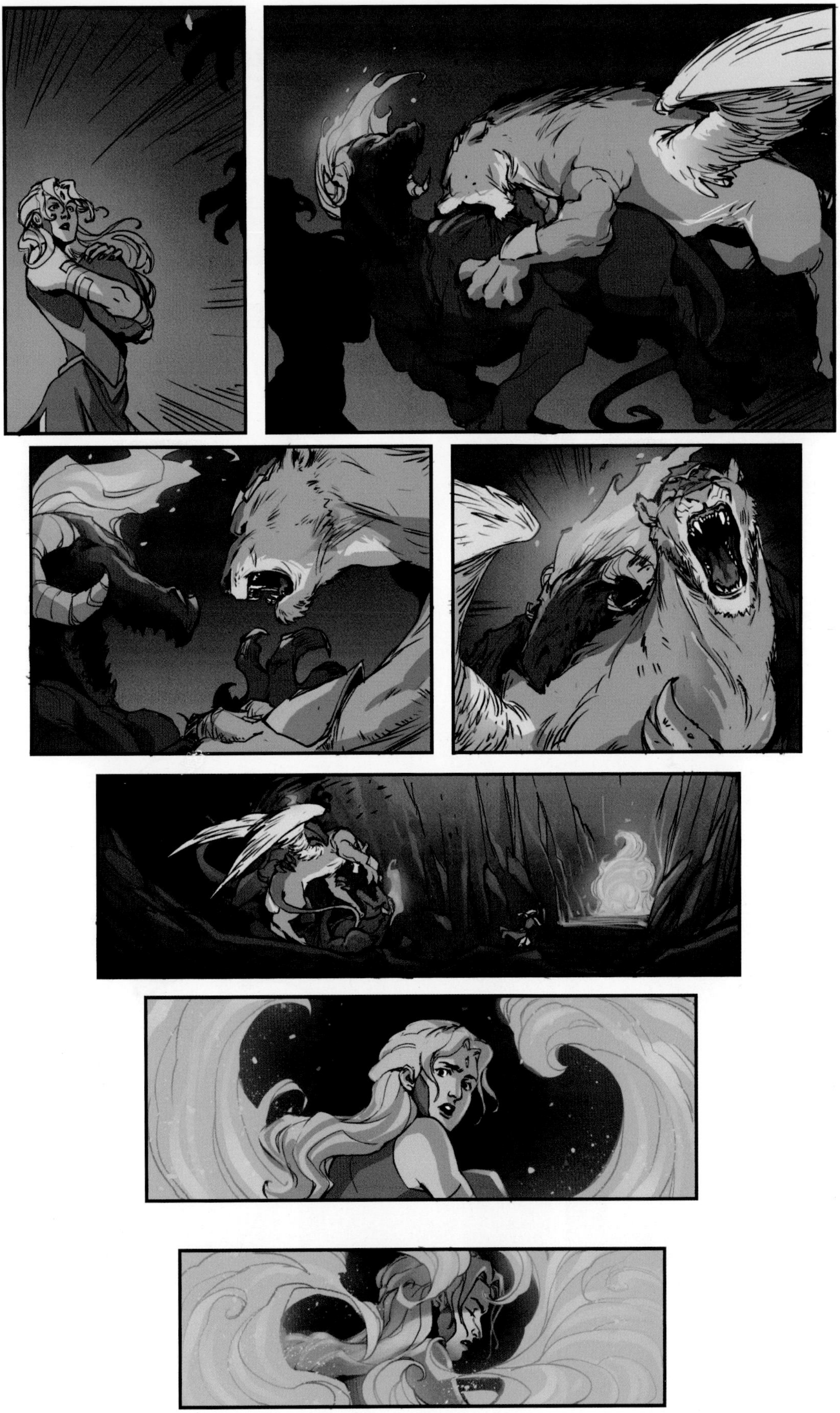

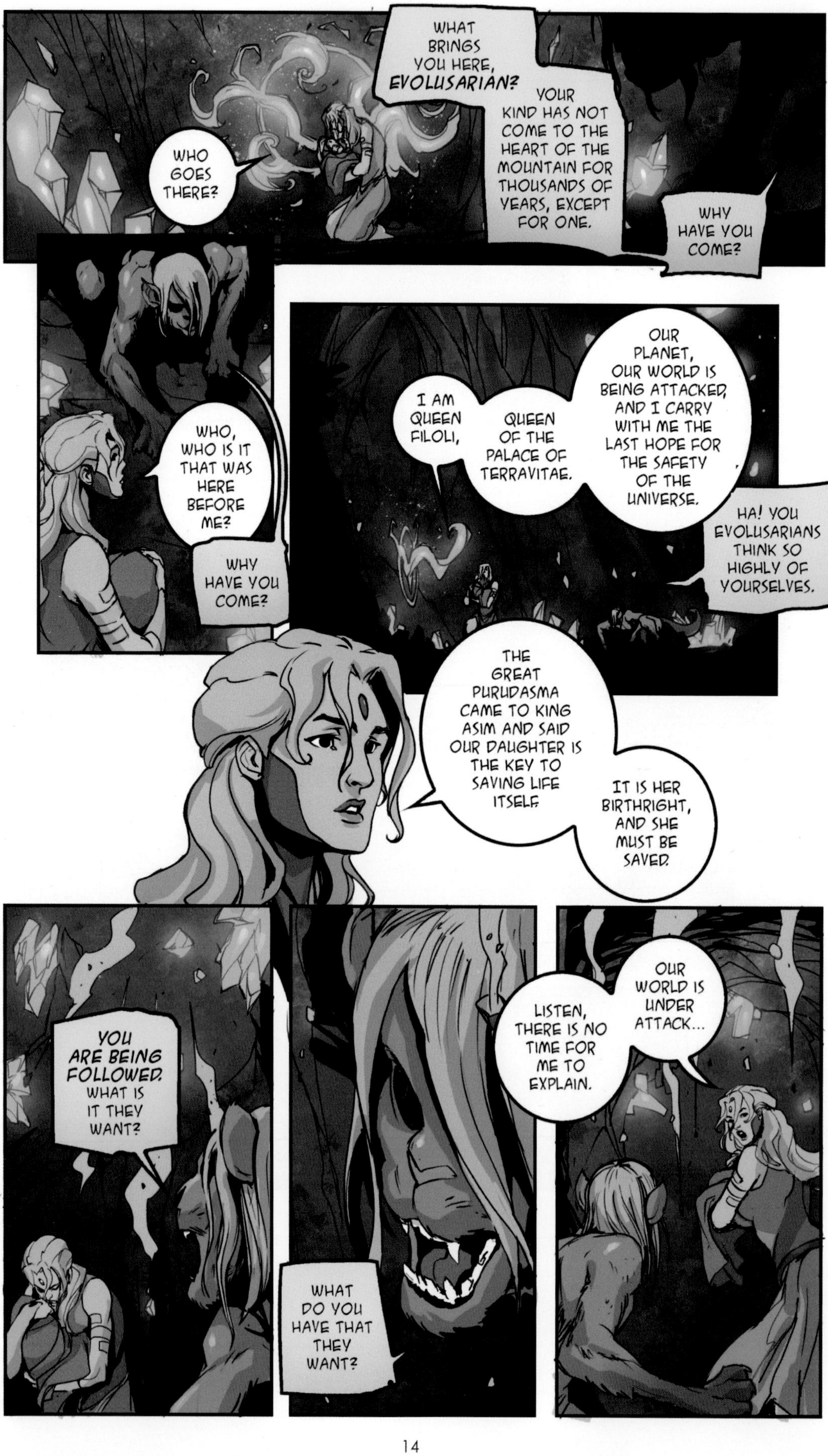
WHAT BRINGS YOU HERE, EVOLUSARIAN?
WHO GOES THERE?
YOUR KIND HAS NOT COME TO THE HEART OF THE MOUNTAIN FOR THOUSANDS OF YEARS, EXCEPT FOR ONE.
WHY HAVE YOU COME?
WHO, WHO IS IT THAT WAS HERE BEFORE ME?
WHY HAVE YOU COME?
I AM QUEEN FILOLI,
QUEEN OF THE PALACE OF TERRAVITAE.
OUR PLANET, OUR WORLD IS BEING ATTACKED, AND I CARRY WITH ME THE LAST HOPE FOR THE SAFETY OF THE UNIVERSE.
HA! YOU EVOLUSARIANS THINK SO HIGHLY OF YOURSELVES.
THE GREAT PURUDASMA CAME TO KING ASIM AND SAID OUR DAUGHTER IS THE KEY TO SAVING LIFE ITSELF.
IT IS HER BIRTHRIGHT, AND SHE MUST BE SAVED.
YOU ARE BEING FOLLOWED. WHAT IS IT THEY WANT?
WHAT DO YOU HAVE THAT THEY WANT?
LISTEN, THERE IS NO TIME FOR ME TO EXPLAIN.
OUR WORLD IS UNDER ATTACK...

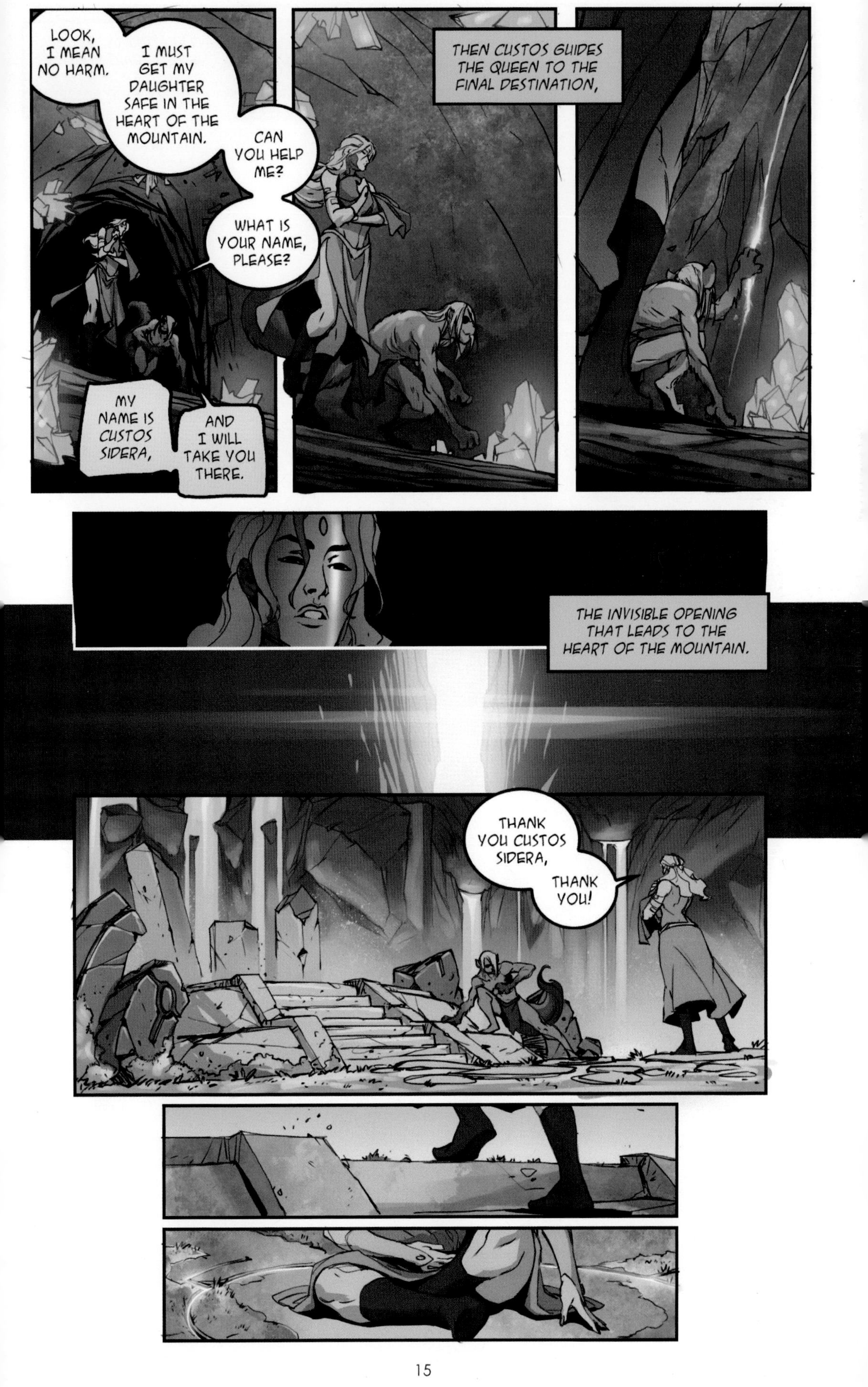
LOOK, I MEAN NO HARM.
I MUST GET MY DAUGHTER SAFE IN THE HEART OF THE MOUNTAIN.
CAN YOU HELP ME?
WHAT IS YOUR NAME, PLEASE?
MY NAME IS CUSTOS SIDERA,
AND I WILL TAKE YOU THERE.
THEN CUSTOS GUIDES THE QUEEN TO THE FINAL DESTINATION,
THE INVISIBLE OPENING THAT LEADS TO THE HEART OF THE MOUNTAIN.
THANK YOU CUSTOS SIDERA,
THANK YOU!

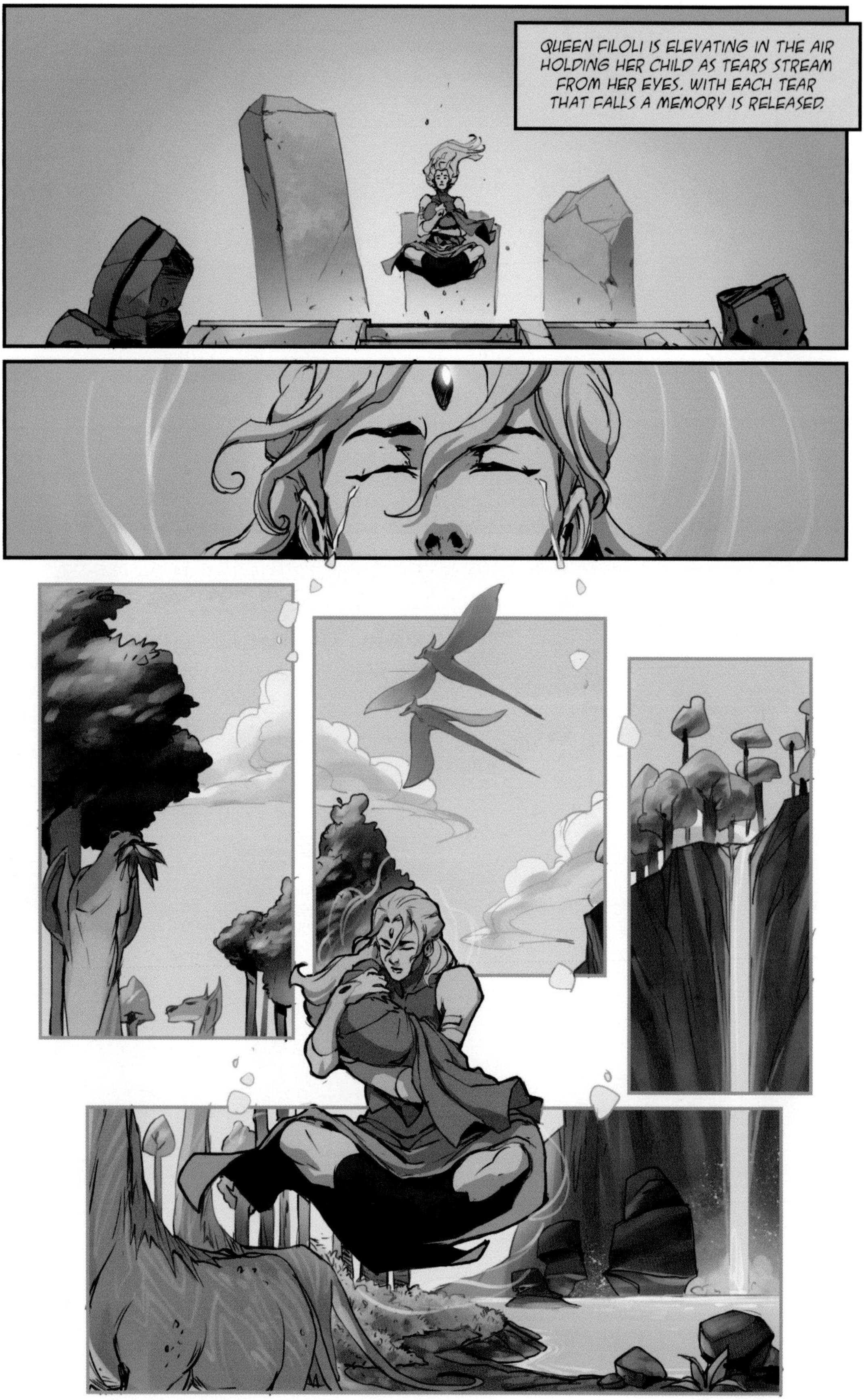
QUEEN FILOLI IS ELEVATING IN THE AIR HOLDING HER CHILD AS TEARS STREAM FROM HER EYES. WITH EACH TEAR THAT FALLS A MEMORY IS RELEASED.

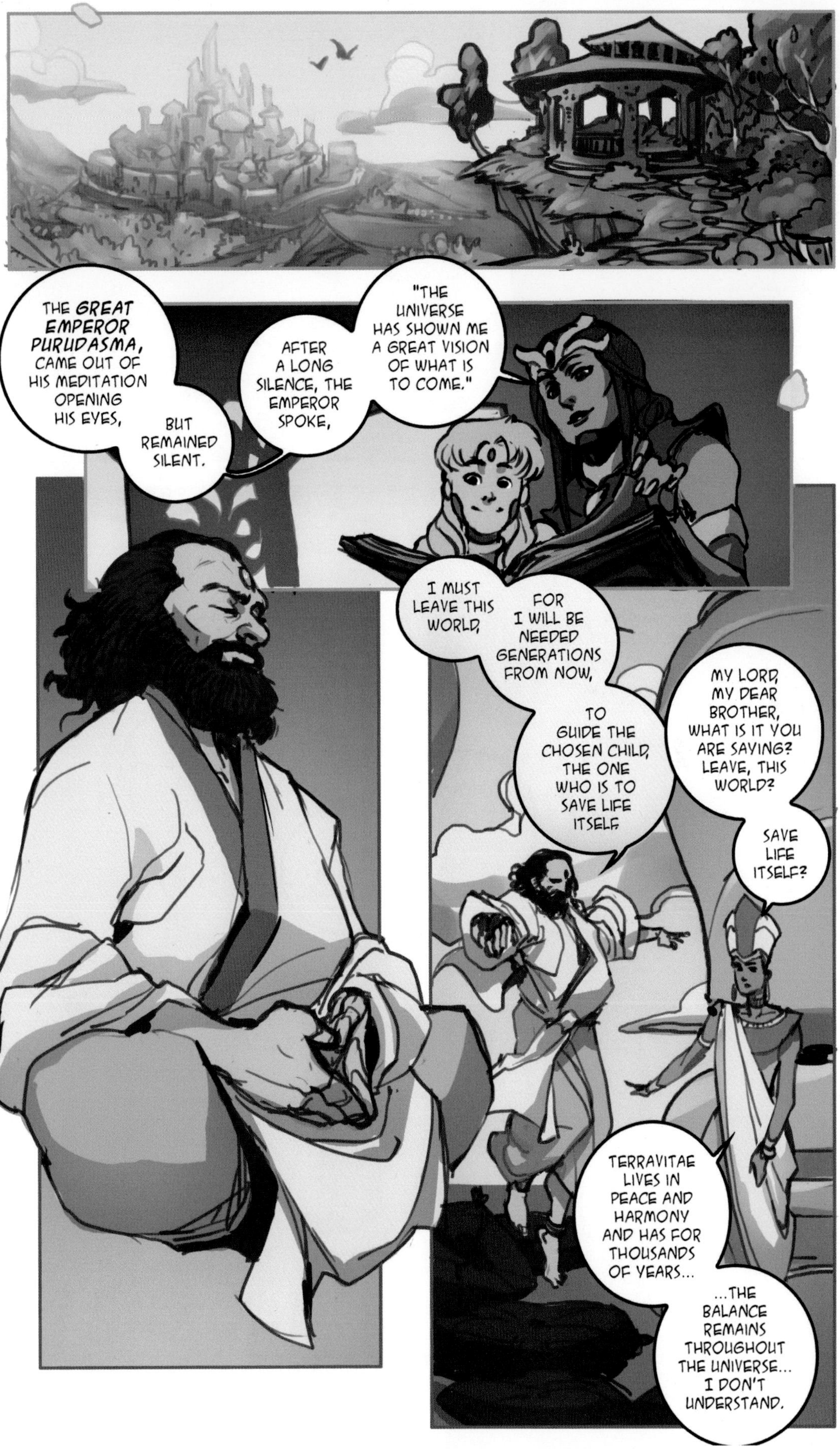
THE GREAT EMPEROR PURUDASMA, CAME OUT OF HIS MEDITATION OPENING HIS EYES,
BUT REMAINED SILENT.
AFTER A LONG SILENCE, THE EMPEROR SPOKE,
"THE UNIVERSE HAS SHOWN ME A GREAT VISION OF WHAT IS TO COME."
I MUST LEAVE THIS WORLD,
FOR I WILL BE NEEDED GENERATIONS FROM NOW,
TO GUIDE THE CHOSEN CHILD, THE ONE WHO IS TO SAVE LIFE ITSELF.
MY LORD, MY DEAR BROTHER, WHAT IS IT YOU ARE SAYING? LEAVE, THIS WORLD?
SAVE LIFE ITSELF?
TERRAVITAE LIVES IN PEACE AND HARMONY AND HAS FOR THOUSANDS OF YEARS...
...THE BALANCE REMAINS THROUGHOUT THE UNIVERSE... I DON'T UNDERSTAND.

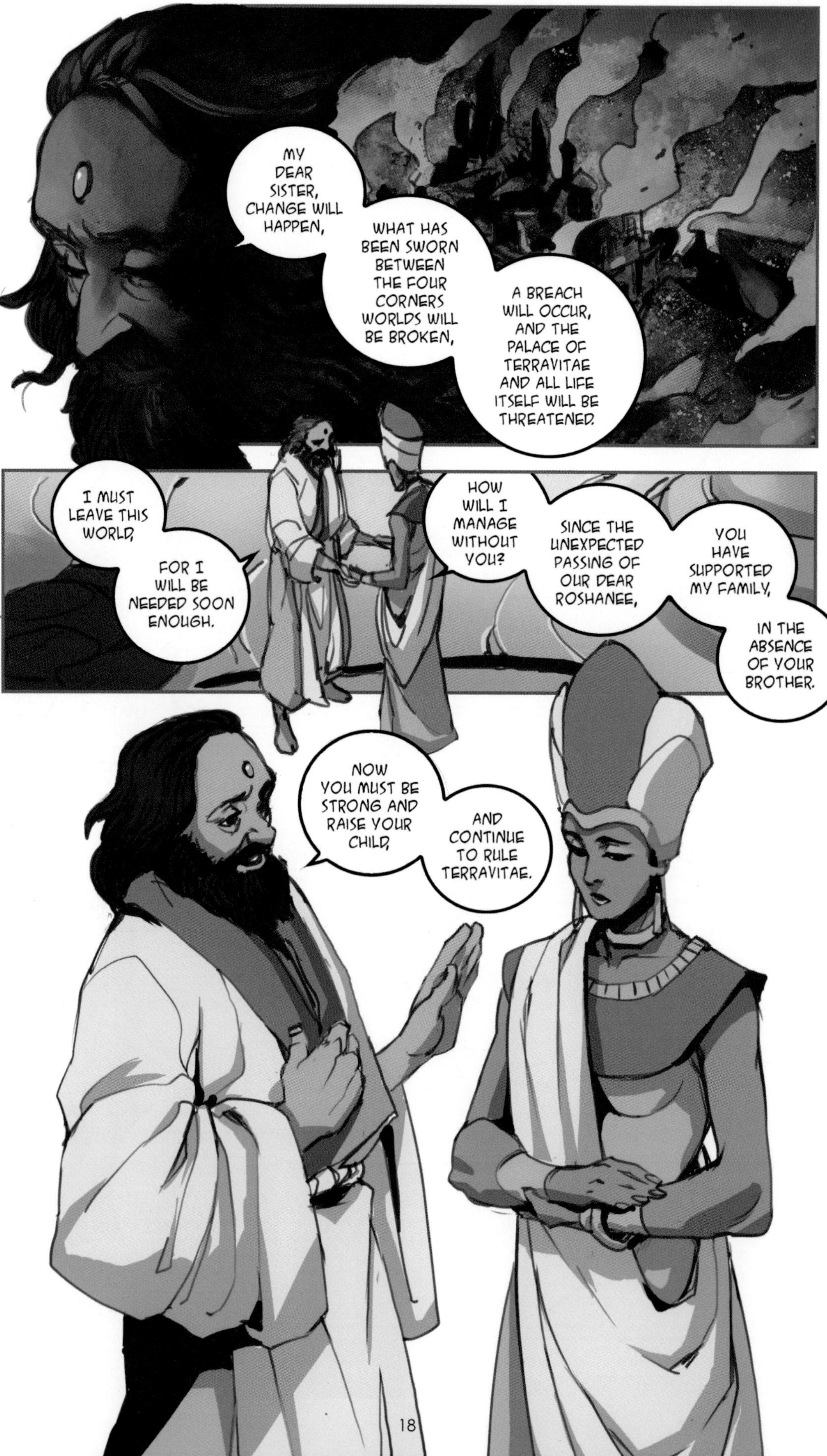
MY DEAR SISTER, CHANGE WILL HAPPEN,
WHAT HAS BEEN SWORN BETWEEN THE FOUR CORNERS WORLDS WILL BE BROKEN,
A BREACH WILL OCCUR, AND THE PALACE OF TERRAVITAE AND ALL LIFE ITSELF WILL BE THREATENED.
I MUST LEAVE THIS WORLD,
FOR I WILL BE NEEDED SOON ENOUGH.
HOW WILL I MANAGE WITHOUT YOU?
SINCE THE UNEXPECTED PASSING OF OUR DEAR ROSHANEE,
YOU HAVE SUPPORTED MY FAMILY,
IN THE ABSENCE OF YOUR BROTHER.
NOW YOU MUST BE STRONG AND RAISE YOUR CHILD,
AND CONTINUE TO RULE TERRAVITAE.

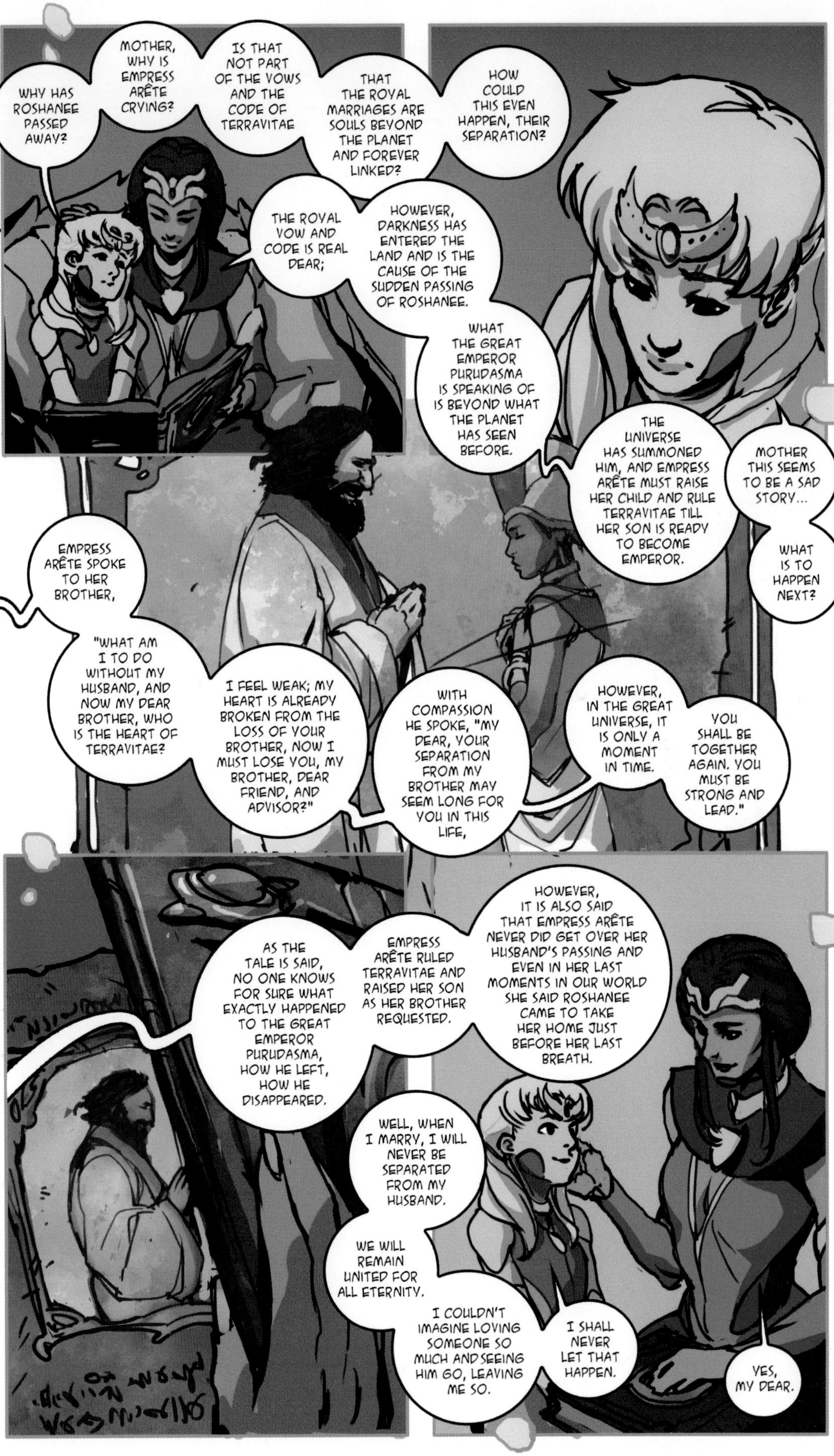
WHY HAS ROSHANEE PASSED AWAY?
MOTHER, WHY IS EMPRESS ARÊTE CRYING?
IS THAT NOT PART OF THE VOWS AND THE CODE OF TERRAVITAE
THAT THE ROYAL MARRIAGES ARE SOULS BEYOND THE PLANET AND FOREVER LINKED?
HOW COULD THIS EVEN HAPPEN, THEIR SEPARATION?
THE ROYAL VOW AND CODE IS REAL DEAR;
HOWEVER, DARKNESS HAS ENTERED THE LAND AND IS THE CAUSE OF THE SUDDEN PASSING OF ROSHANEE.
WHAT THE GREAT EMPEROR PURUDASMA IS SPEAKING OF IS BEYOND WHAT THE PLANET HAS SEEN BEFORE.
THE UNIVERSE HAS SUMMONED HIM, AND EMPRESS ARÊTE MUST RAISE HER CHILD AND RULE TERRAVITAE TILL HER SON IS READY TO BECOME EMPEROR.
MOTHER THIS SEEMS TO BE A SAD STORY...
WHAT IS TO HAPPEN NEXT?
EMPRESS ARÊTE SPOKE TO HER BROTHER,
"WHAT AM I TO DO WITHOUT MY HUSBAND, AND NOW MY DEAR BROTHER, WHO IS THE HEART OF TERRAVITAE?
I FEEL WEAK; MY HEART IS ALREADY BROKEN FROM THE LOSS OF YOUR BROTHER, NOW I MUST LOSE YOU, MY BROTHER, DEAR FRIEND, AND ADVISOR?"
WITH COMPASSION HE SPOKE, "MY DEAR, YOUR SEPARATION FROM MY BROTHER MAY SEEM LONG FOR YOU IN THIS LIFE,
HOWEVER, IN THE GREAT UNIVERSE, IT IS ONLY A MOMENT IN TIME.
YOU SHALL BE TOGETHER AGAIN. YOU MUST BE STRONG AND LEAD."
AS THE TALE IS SAID, NO ONE KNOWS FOR SURE WHAT EXACTLY HAPPENED TO THE GREAT EMPEROR PURUDASMA, HOW HE LEFT, HOW HE DISAPPEARED.
EMPRESS ARÊTE RULED TERRAVITAE AND RAISED HER SON AS HER BROTHER REQUESTED.
HOWEVER, IT IS ALSO SAID THAT EMPRESS ARÊTE NEVER DID GET OVER HER HUSBAND'S PASSING AND EVEN IN HER LAST MOMENTS IN OUR WORLD SHE SAID ROSHANEE CAME TO TAKE HER HOME JUST BEFORE HER LAST BREATH.
WELL, WHEN I MARRY, I WILL NEVER BE SEPARATED FROM MY HUSBAND.
WE WILL REMAIN UNITED FOR ALL ETERNITY.
I COULDN'T IMAGINE LOVING SOMEONE SO MUCH AND SEEING HIM GO, LEAVING ME SO.
I SHALL NEVER LET THAT HAPPEN.
YES, MY DEAR.

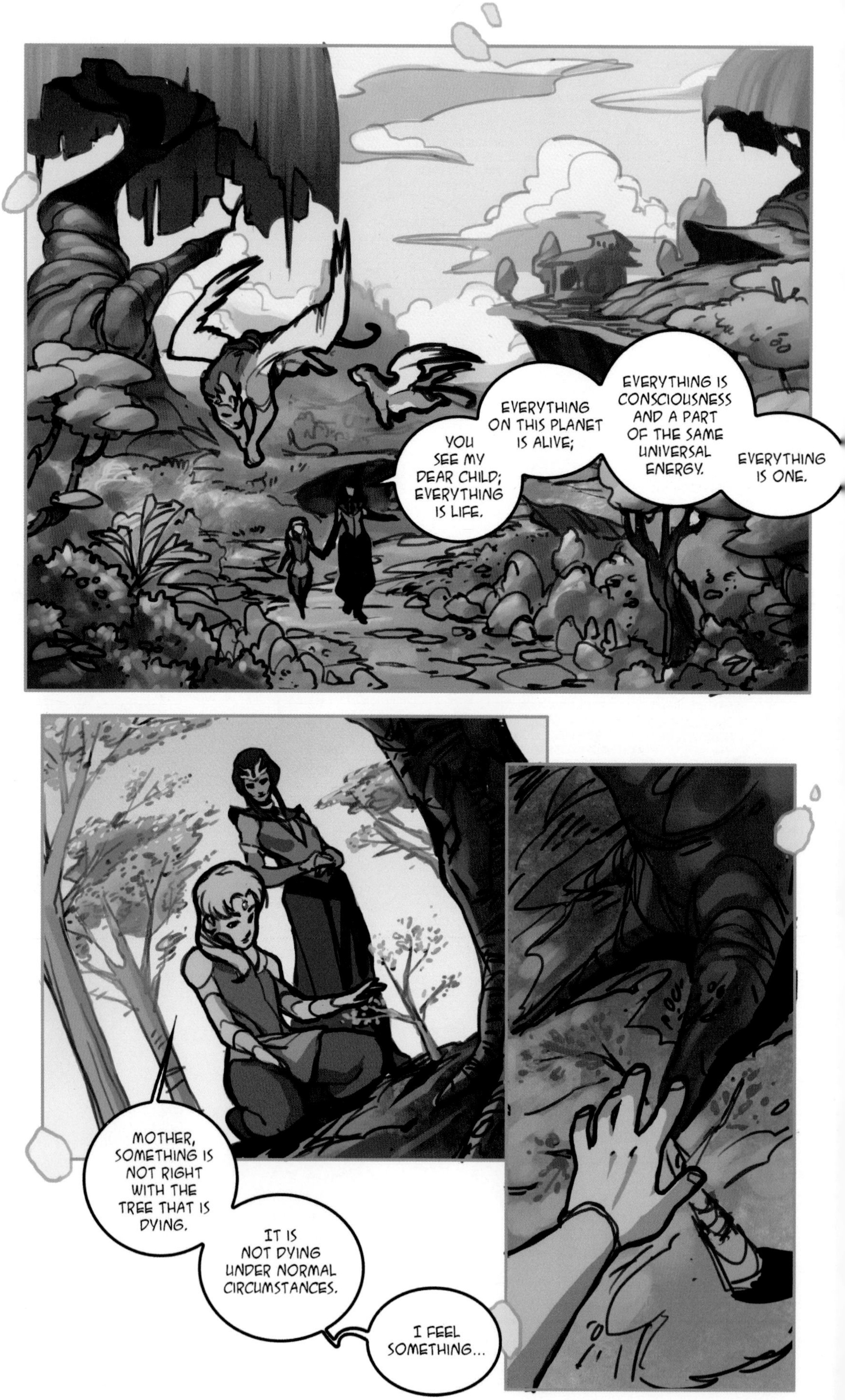
YOU SEE MY DEAR CHILD; EVERYTHING IS LIFE.
EVERYTHING ON THIS PLANET IS ALIVE;
EVERYTHING IS CONSCIOUSNESS AND A PART OF THE SAME UNIVERSAL ENERGY.
EVERYTHING IS ONE.
MOTHER, SOMETHING IS NOT RIGHT WITH THE TREE THAT IS DYING.
IT IS NOT DYING UNDER NORMAL CIRCUMSTANCES.
I FEEL SOMETHING...

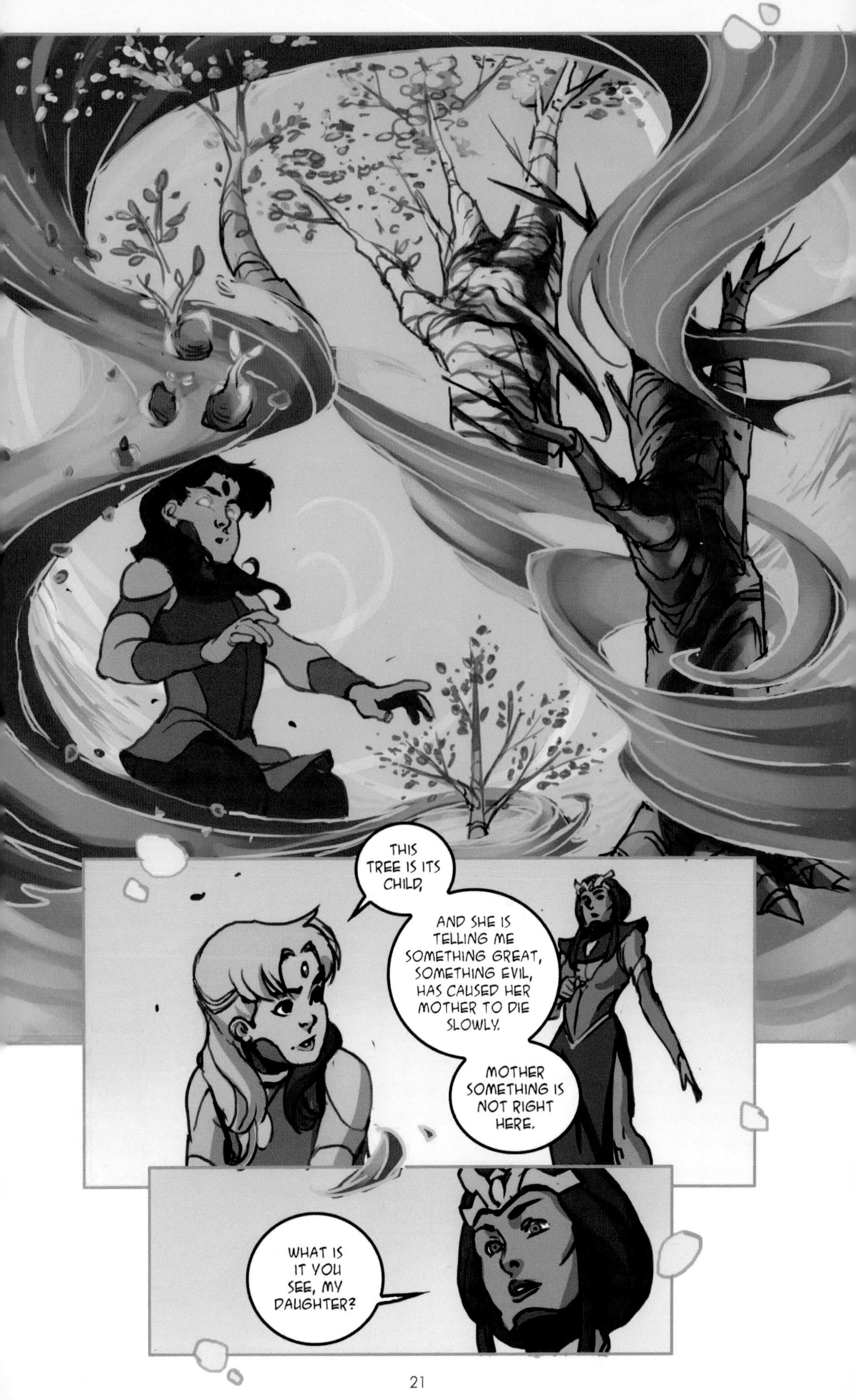

THIS TREE IS ITS CHILD,
AND SHE IS TELLING ME SOMETHING GREAT, SOMETHING EVIL, HAS CAUSED HER MOTHER TO DIE SLOWLY.
MOTHER SOMETHING IS NOT RIGHT HERE.
WHAT IS IT YOU SEE, MY DAUGHTER?

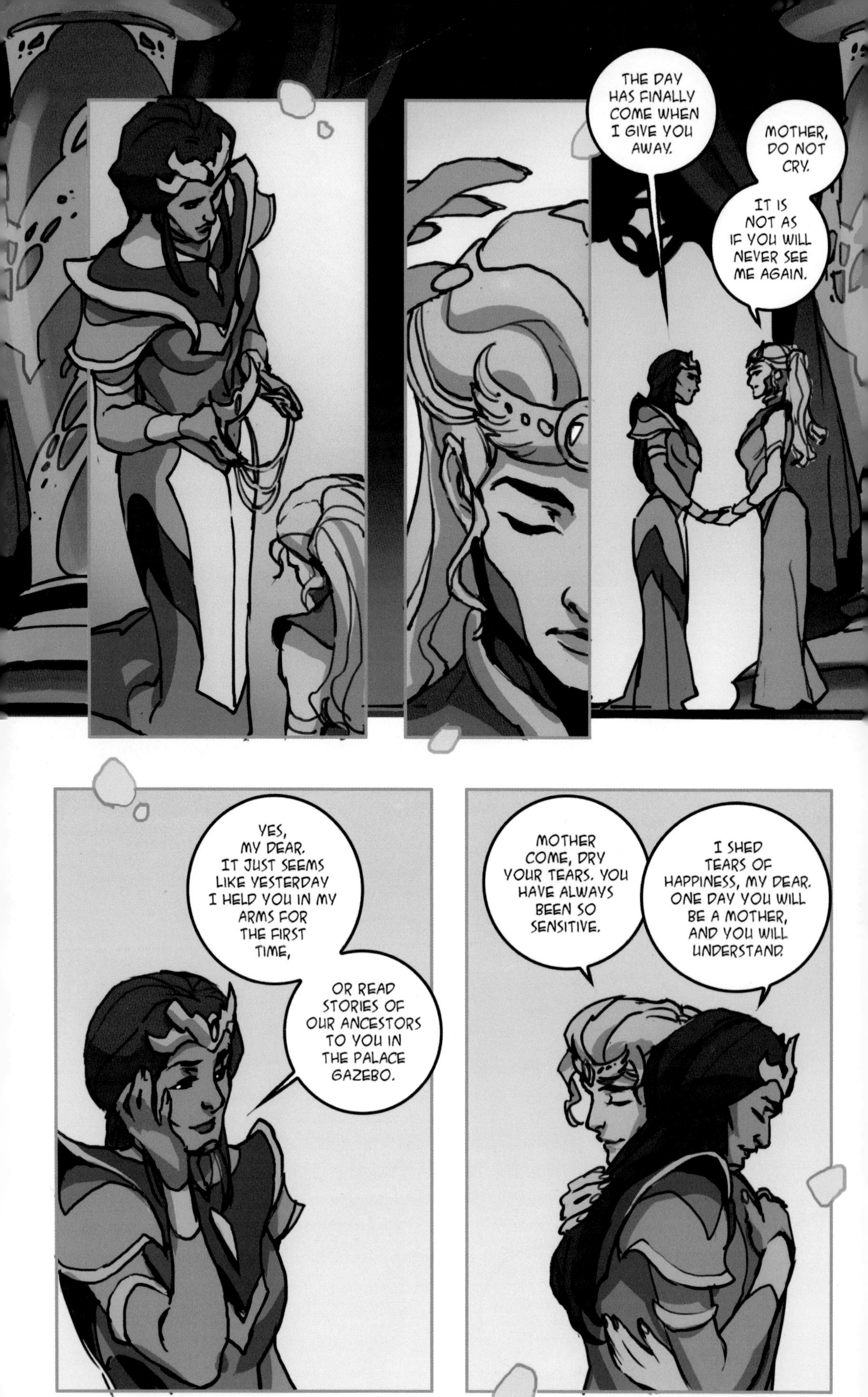
THE DAY HAS FINALLY COME WHEN I GIVE YOU AWAY.
MOTHER, DO NOT CRY.
IT IS NOT AS IF YOU WILL NEVER SEE ME AGAIN.
YES, MY DEAR. IT JUST SEEMS LIKE YESTERDAY I HELD YOU IN MY ARMS FOR THE FIRST TIME,
OR READ STORIES OF OUR ANCESTORS TO YOU IN THE PALACE GAZEBO.
MOTHER COME, DRY YOUR TEARS. YOU HAVE ALWAYS BEEN SO SENSITIVE.
I SHED TEARS OF HAPPINESS, MY DEAR. ONE DAY YOU WILL BE A MOTHER, AND YOU WILL UNDERSTAND.

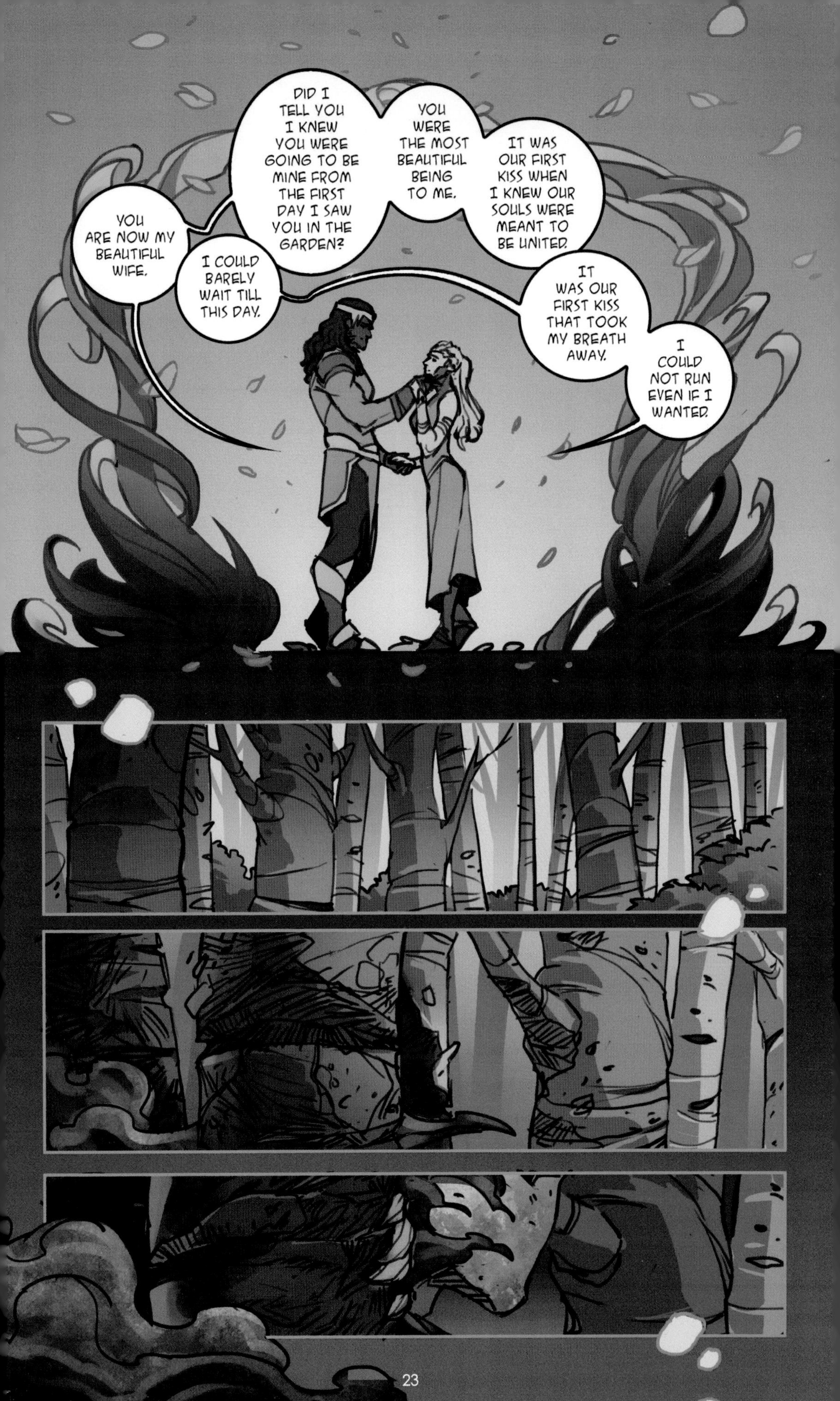

YOU ARE NOW MY BEAUTIFUL WIFE.
I COULD BARELY WAIT TILL THIS DAY.
DID I TELL YOU I KNEW YOU WERE GOING TO BE MINE FROM THE FIRST DAY I SAW YOU IN THE GARDEN?
YOU WERE THE MOST BEAUTIFUL BEING TO ME.
IT WAS OUR FIRST KISS WHEN I KNEW OUR SOULS WERE MEANT TO BE UNITED.
IT WAS OUR FIRST KISS THAT TOOK MY BREATH AWAY.
I COULD NOT RUN EVEN IF I WANTED.

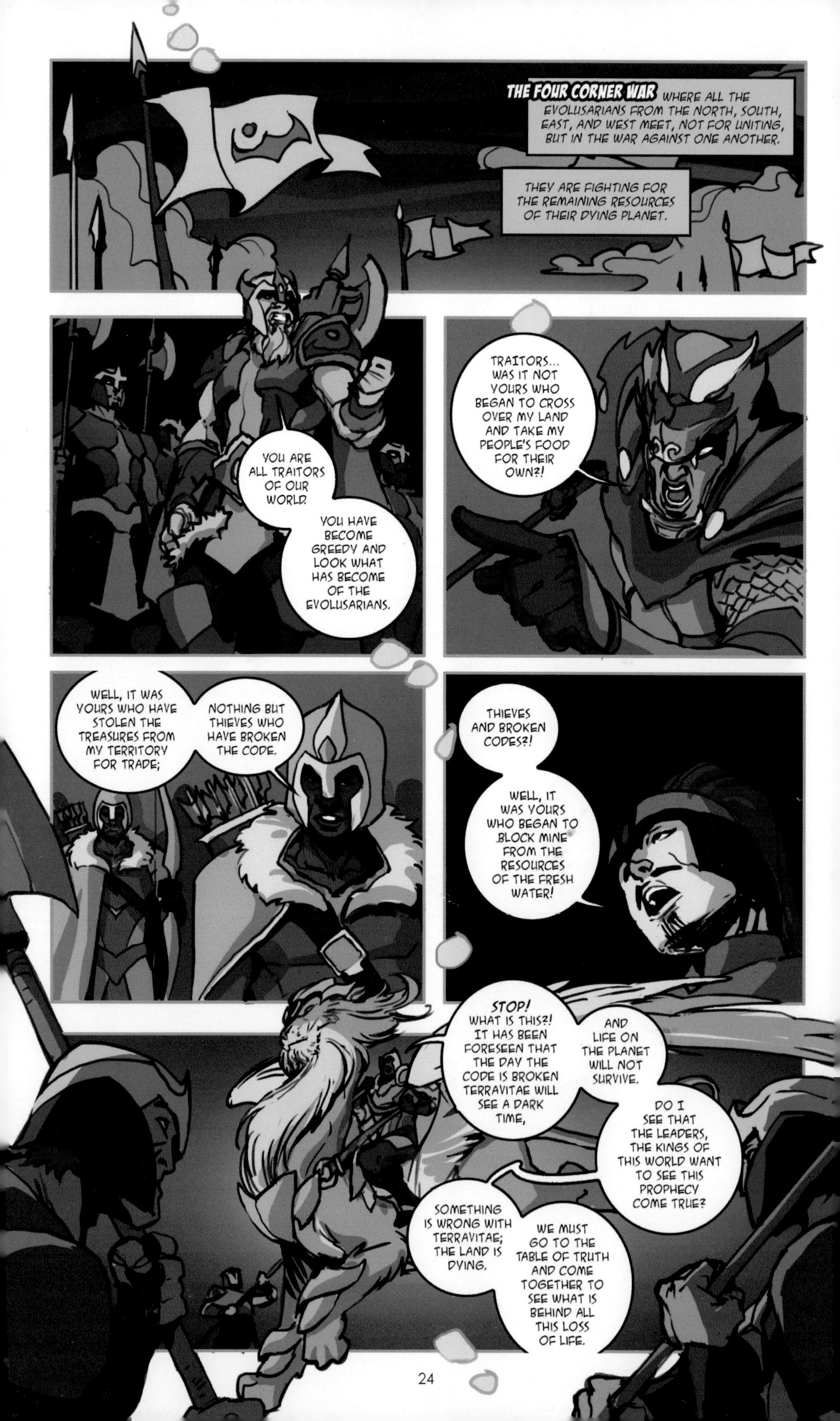
THE FOUR CORNER WAR WHERE ALL THE EVOLUSARIANS FROM THE NORTH, SOUTH, EAST, AND WEST MEET, NOT FOR UNITING, BUT IN THE WAR AGAINST ONE ANOTHER.
THEY ARE FIGHTING FOR THE REMAINING RESOURCES OF THEIR DYING PLANET.
YOU ARE ALL TRAITORS OF OUR WORLD.
YOU HAVE BECOME GREEDY AND LOOK WHAT HAS BECOME OF THE EVOLUSARIANS.
TRAITORS... WAS IT NOT YOURS WHO BEGAN TO CROSS OVER MY LAND AND TAKE MY PEOPLE'S FOOD FOR THEIR OWN?!
WELL, IT WAS YOURS WHO HAVE STOLEN THE TREASURES FROM MY TERRITORY FOR TRADE;
NOTHING BUT THIEVES WHO HAVE BROKEN THE CODE.
THIEVES AND BROKEN CODES?!
WELL, IT WAS YOURS WHO BEGAN TO BLOCK MINE FROM THE RESOURCES OF THE FRESH WATER!
STOP! WHAT IS THIS?! IT HAS BEEN FORESEEN THAT THE DAY THE CODE IS BROKEN TERRAVITAE WILL SEE A DARK TIME,
AND LIFE ON THE PLANET WILL NOT SURVIVE.
DO I SEE THAT THE LEADERS, THE KINGS OF THIS WORLD WANT TO SEE THIS PROPHECY COME TRUE?
SOMETHING IS WRONG WITH TERRAVITAE; THE LAND IS DYING.
WE MUST GO TO THE TABLE OF TRUTH AND COME TOGETHER TO SEE WHAT IS BEHIND ALL THIS LOSS OF LIFE.

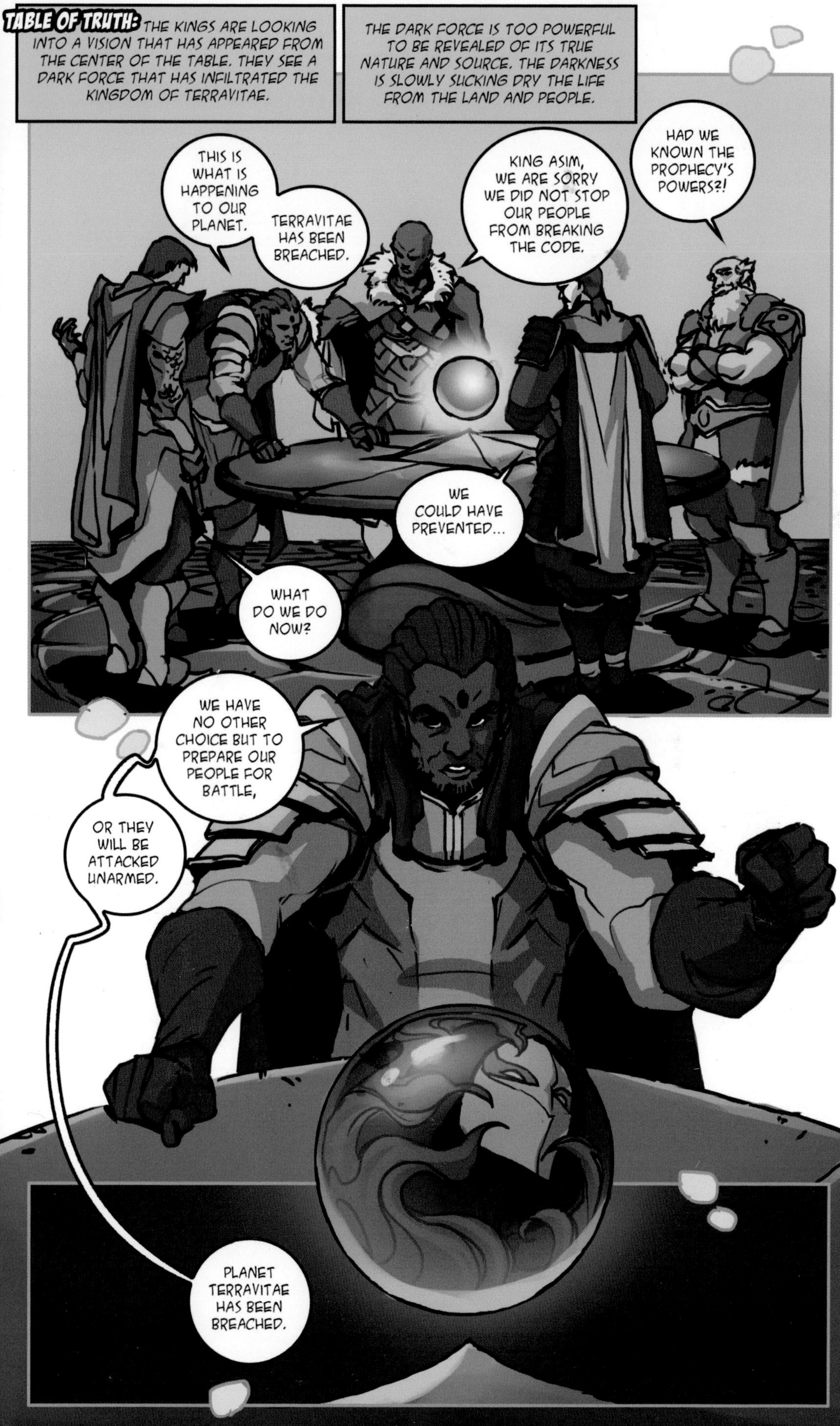
TABLE OF TRUTH: THE KINGS ARE LOOKING INTO A VISION THAT HAS APPEARED FROM THE CENTER OF THE TABLE. THEY SEE A DARK FORCE THAT HAS INFILTRATED THE KINGDOM OF TERRAVITAE.
THE DARK FORCE IS TOO POWERFUL TO BE REVEALED OF ITS TRUE NATURE AND SOURCE. THE DARKNESS IS SLOWLY SUCKING DRY THE LIFE FROM THE LAND AND PEOPLE.
THIS IS WHAT IS HAPPENING TO OUR PLANET.
TERRAVITAE HAS BEEN BREACHED.
KING ASIM, WE ARE SORRY WE DID NOT STOP OUR PEOPLE FROM BREAKING THE CODE.
HAD WE KNOWN THE PROPHECY'S POWERS?!
WE COULD HAVE PREVENTED...
WHAT DO WE DO NOW?
WE HAVE NO OTHER CHOICE BUT TO PREPARE OUR PEOPLE FOR BATTLE,
OR THEY WILL BE ATTACKED UNARMED.
PLANET TERRAVITAE HAS BEEN BREACHED.

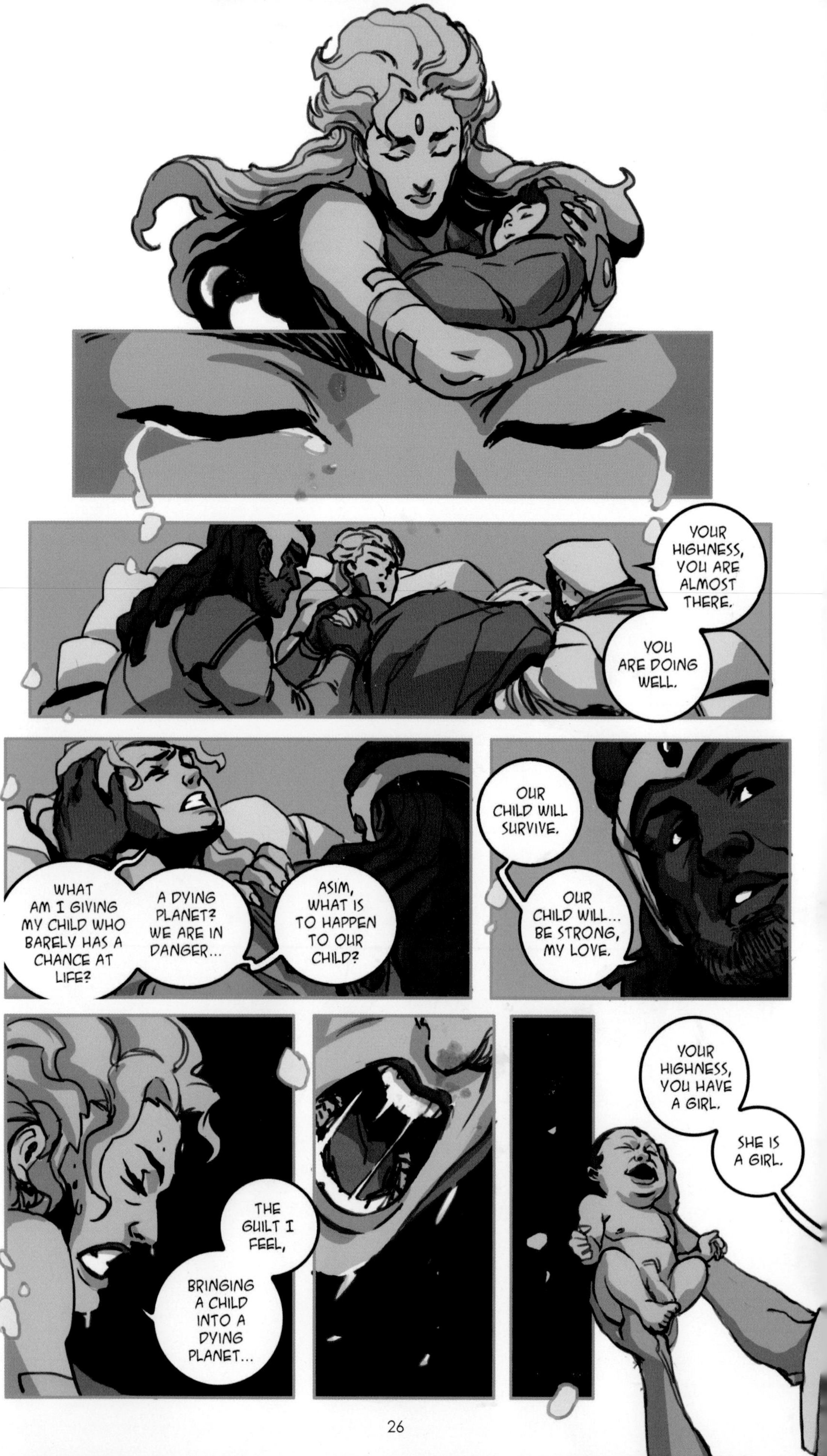
YOUR HIGHNESS, YOU ARE ALMOST THERE.
YOU ARE DOING WELL.
WHAT AM I GIVING MY CHILD WHO BARELY HAS A CHANCE AT LIFE?
A DYING PLANET? WE ARE IN DANGER...
ASIM, WHAT IS TO HAPPEN TO OUR CHILD?
OUR CHILD WILL SURVIVE.
OUR CHILD WILL... BE STRONG, MY LOVE.
THE GUILT I FEEL,
BRINGING A CHILD INTO A DYING PLANET...
YOUR HIGHNESS, YOU HAVE A GIRL.
SHE IS A GIRL.

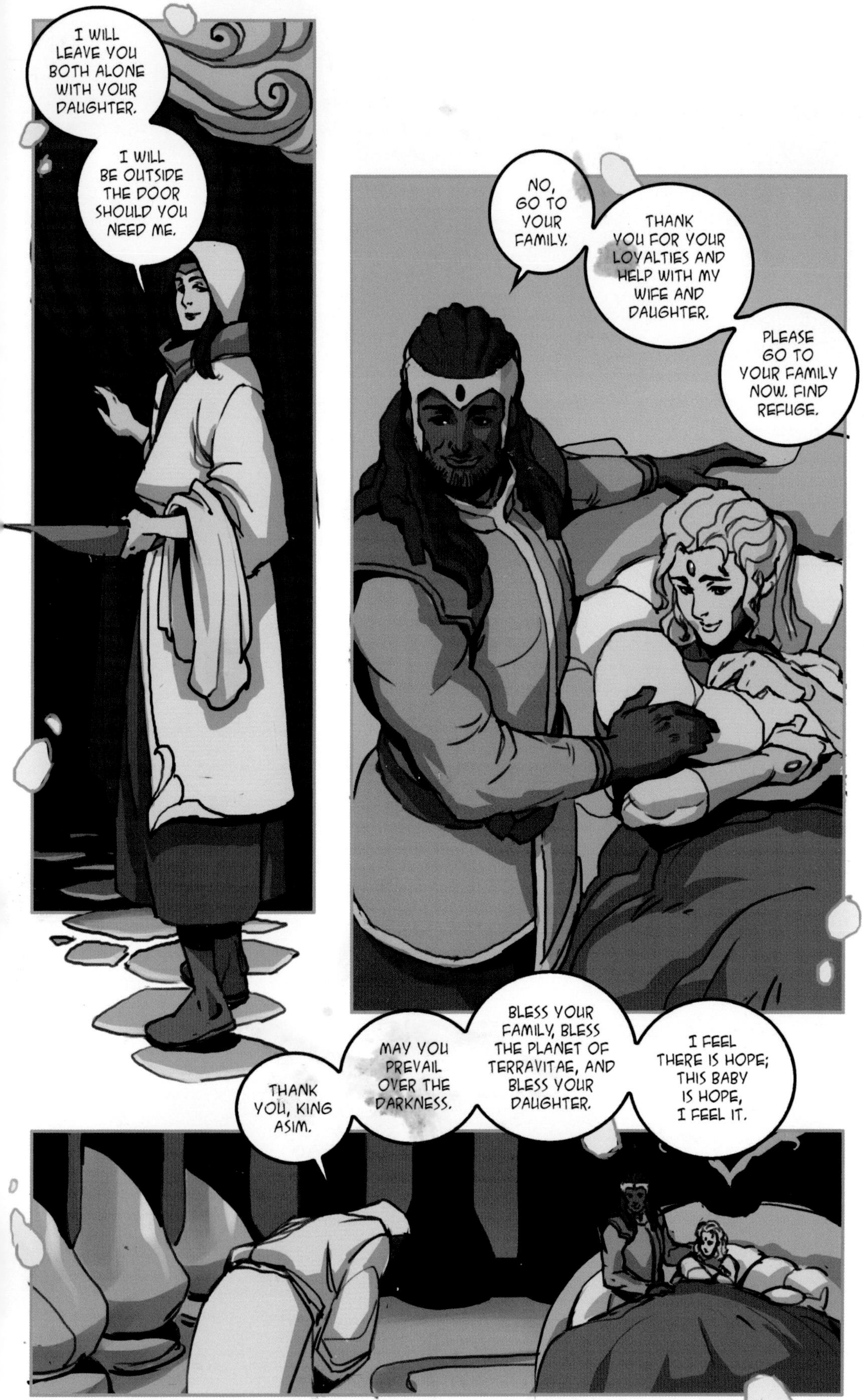

I WILL LEAVE YOU BOTH ALONE WITH YOUR DAUGHTER.
I WILL BE OUTSIDE THE DOOR SHOULD YOU NEED ME.
NO, GO TO YOUR FAMILY.
THANK YOU FOR YOUR LOYALTIES AND HELP WITH MY WIFE AND DAUGHTER.
PLEASE GO TO YOUR FAMILY NOW. FIND REFUGE.
THANK YOU, KING ASIM.
MAY YOU PREVAIL OVER THE DARKNESS.
BLESS YOUR FAMILY, BLESS THE PLANET OF TERRAVITAE, AND BLESS YOUR DAUGHTER.
I FEEL THERE IS HOPE; THIS BABY IS HOPE, I FEEL IT.

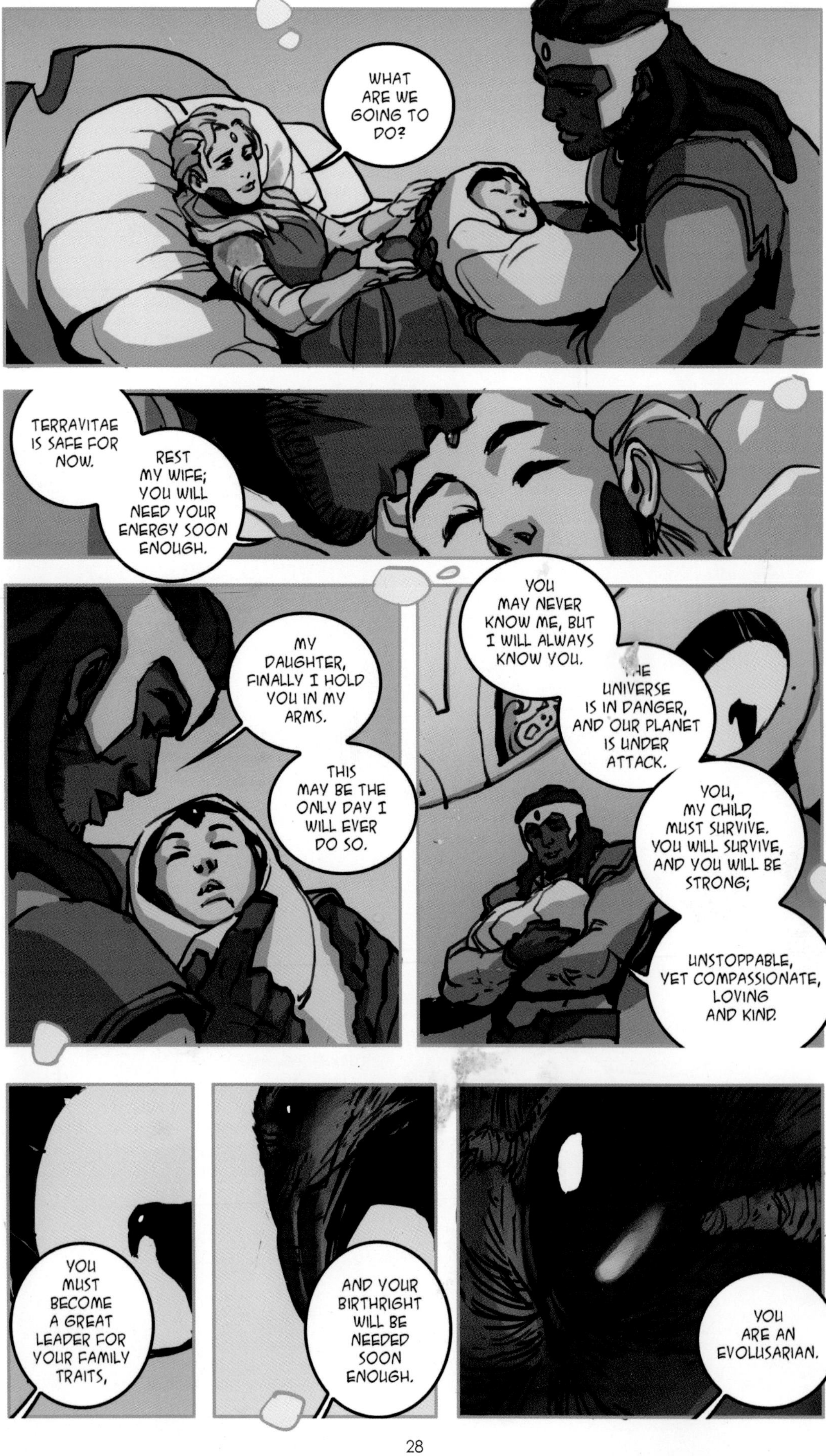
WHAT ARE WE GOING TO DO?
TERRAVITAE IS SAFE FOR NOW.
REST MY WIFE; YOU WILL NEED YOUR ENERGY SOON ENOUGH.
MY DAUGHTER, FINALLY I HOLD YOU IN MY ARMS.
THIS MAY BE THE ONLY DAY I WILL EVER DO SO.
YOU MAY NEVER KNOW ME, BUT I WILL ALWAYS KNOW YOU.
HE UNIVERSE IS IN DANGER, AND OUR PLANET IS UNDER ATTACK.
YOU, MY CHILD, MUST SURVIVE. YOU WILL SURVIVE, AND YOU WILL BE STRONG;
UNSTOPPABLE, YET COMPASSIONATE, LOVING AND KIND.
YOU MUST BECOME A GREAT LEADER FOR YOUR FAMILY TRAITS,
AND YOUR BIRTHRIGHT WILL BE NEEDED SOON ENOUGH.
YOU ARE AN EVOLUSARIAN.

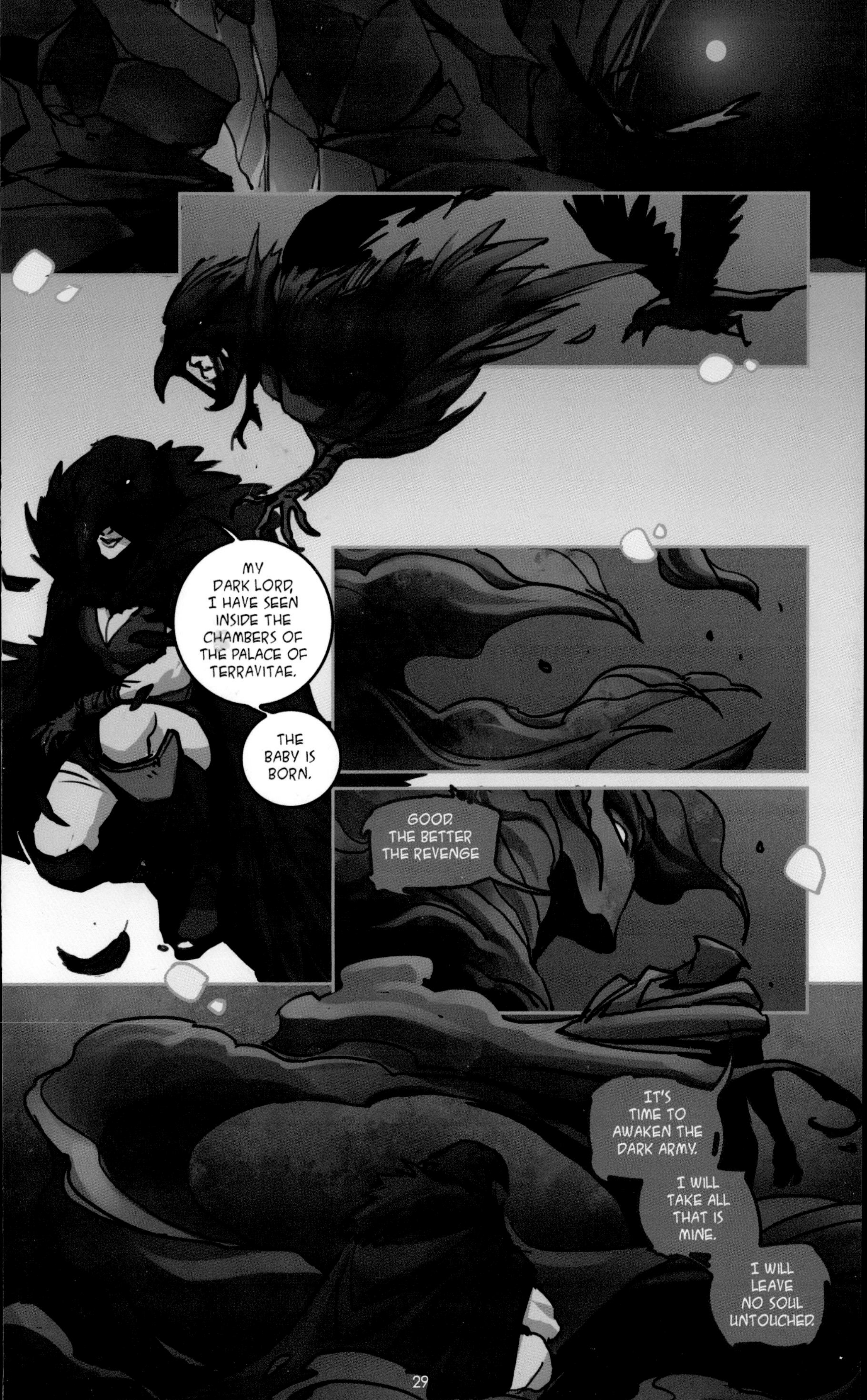
MY DARK LORD, I HAVE SEEN INSIDE THE CHAMBERS OF THE PALACE OF TERRAVITAE.
THE BABY IS BORN.
GOOD. THE BETTER THE REVENGE
IT'S TIME TO AWAKEN THE DARK ARMY.
I WILL TAKE ALL THAT IS MINE.
I WILL LEAVE NO SOUL UNTOUCHED.

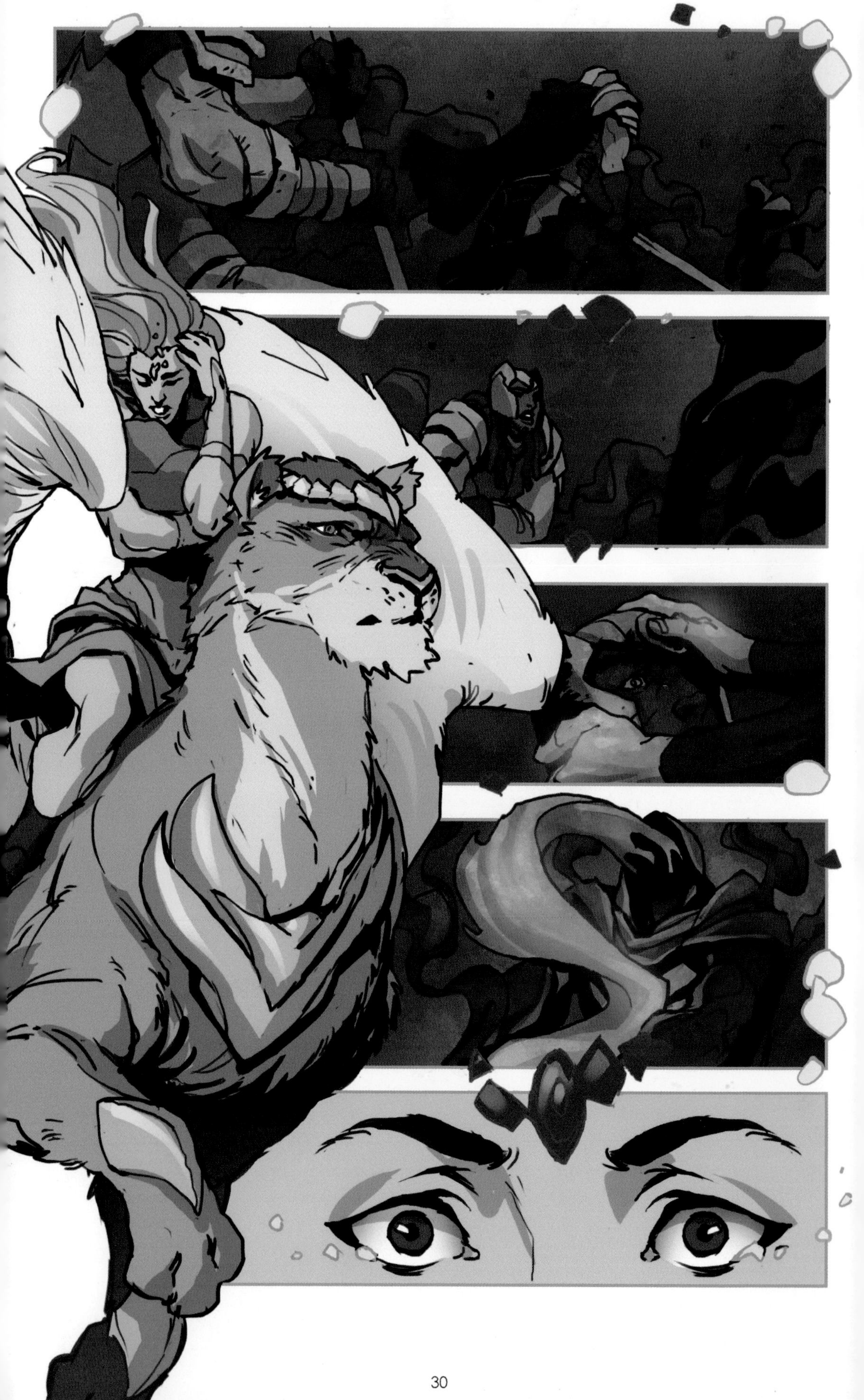

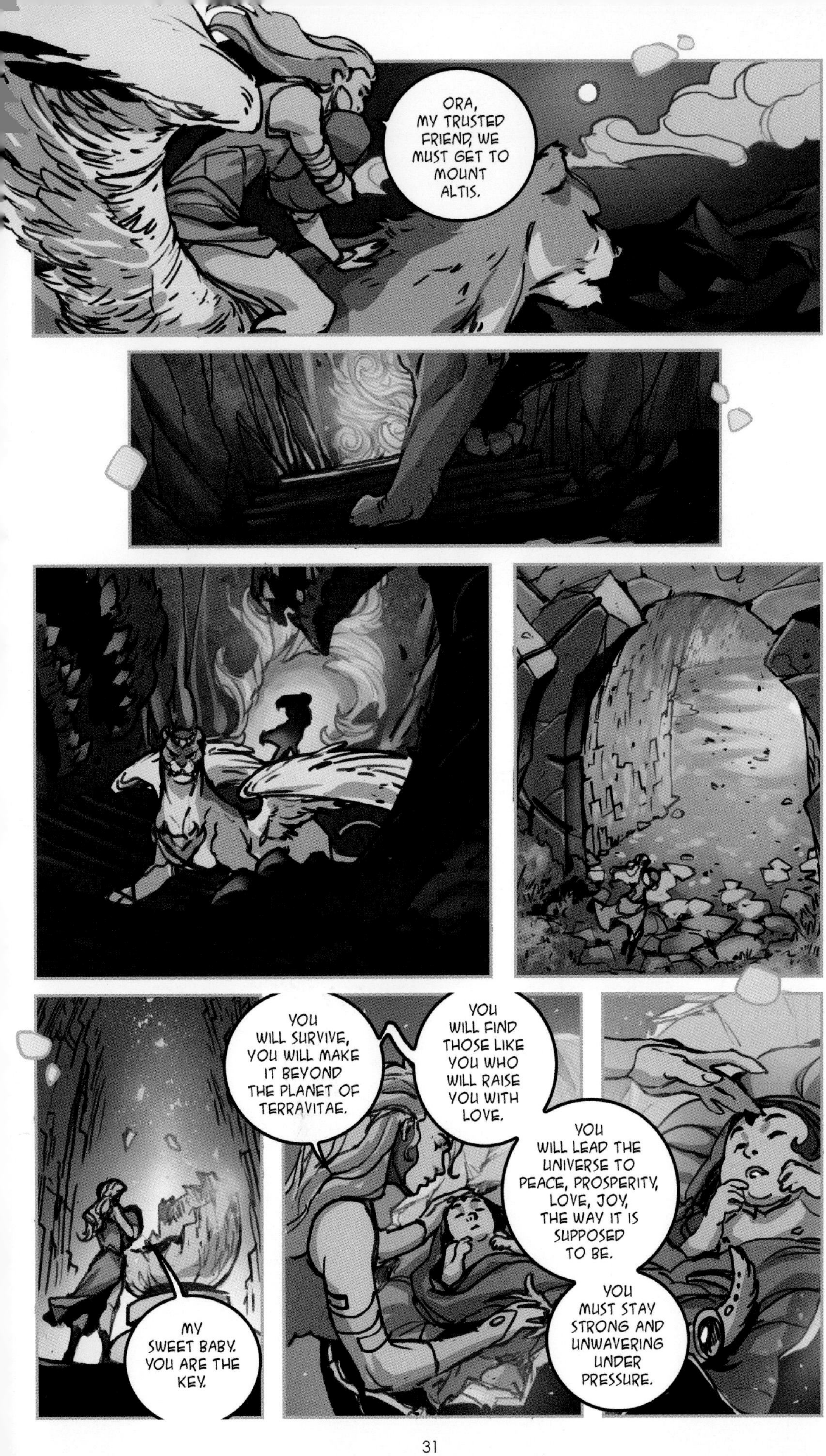
ORA, MY TRUSTED FRIEND, WE MUST GET TO MOUNT ALTIS.
MY SWEET BABY. YOU ARE THE KEY.
YOU WILL SURVIVE, YOU WILL MAKE IT BEYOND THE PLANET OF TERRAVITAE.
YOU WILL FIND THOSE LIKE YOU WHO WILL RAISE YOU WITH LOVE.
YOU WILL LEAD THE UNIVERSE TO PEACE, PROSPERITY, LOVE, JOY, THE WAY IT IS SUPPOSED TO BE.
YOU MUST STAY STRONG AND UNWAVERING UNDER PRESSURE.

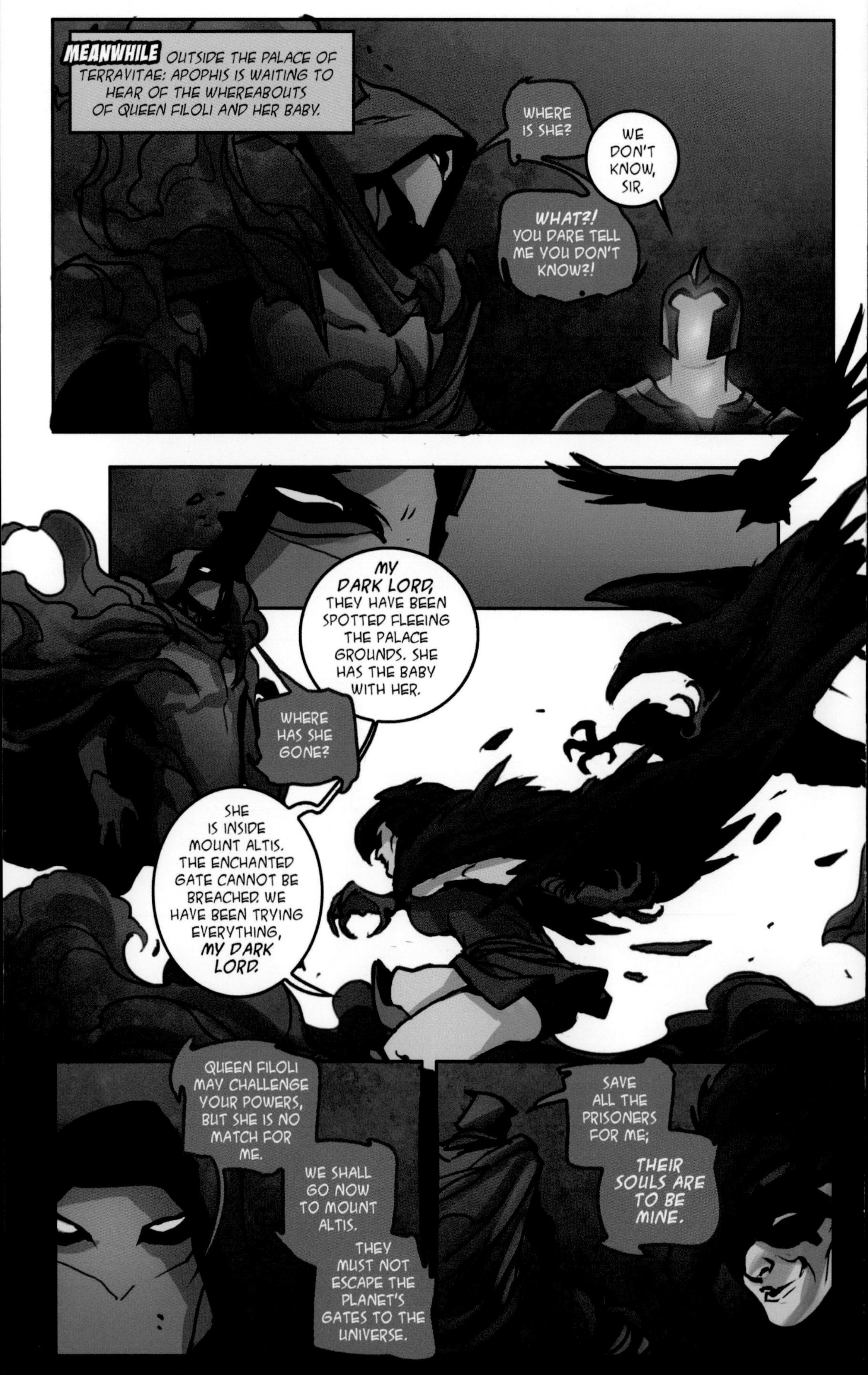
MEANWHILE OUTSIDE THE PALACE OF TERRAVITAE: APOPHIS IS WAITING TO HEAR OF THE WHEREABOUTS OF QUEEN FILOLI AND HER BABY.
WHERE IS SHE?
WE DON'T KNOW, SIR.
WHAT?! YOU DARE TELL ME YOU DON'T KNOW?!
MY DARK LORD, THEY HAVE BEEN SPOTTED FLEEING THE PALACE GROUNDS. SHE HAS THE BABY WITH HER.
WHERE HAS SHE GONE?
SHE IS INSIDE MOUNT ALTIS. THE ENCHANTED GATE CANNOT BE BREACHED. WE HAVE BEEN TRYING EVERYTHING, MY DARK LORD.
QUEEN FILOLI MAY CHALLENGE YOUR POWERS, BUT SHE IS NO MATCH FOR ME.
WE SHALL GO NOW TO MOUNT ALTIS.
THEY MUST NOT ESCAPE THE PLANET'S GATES TO THE UNIVERSE.
SAVE ALL THE PRISONERS FOR ME;
THEIR SOULS ARE TO BE MINE.

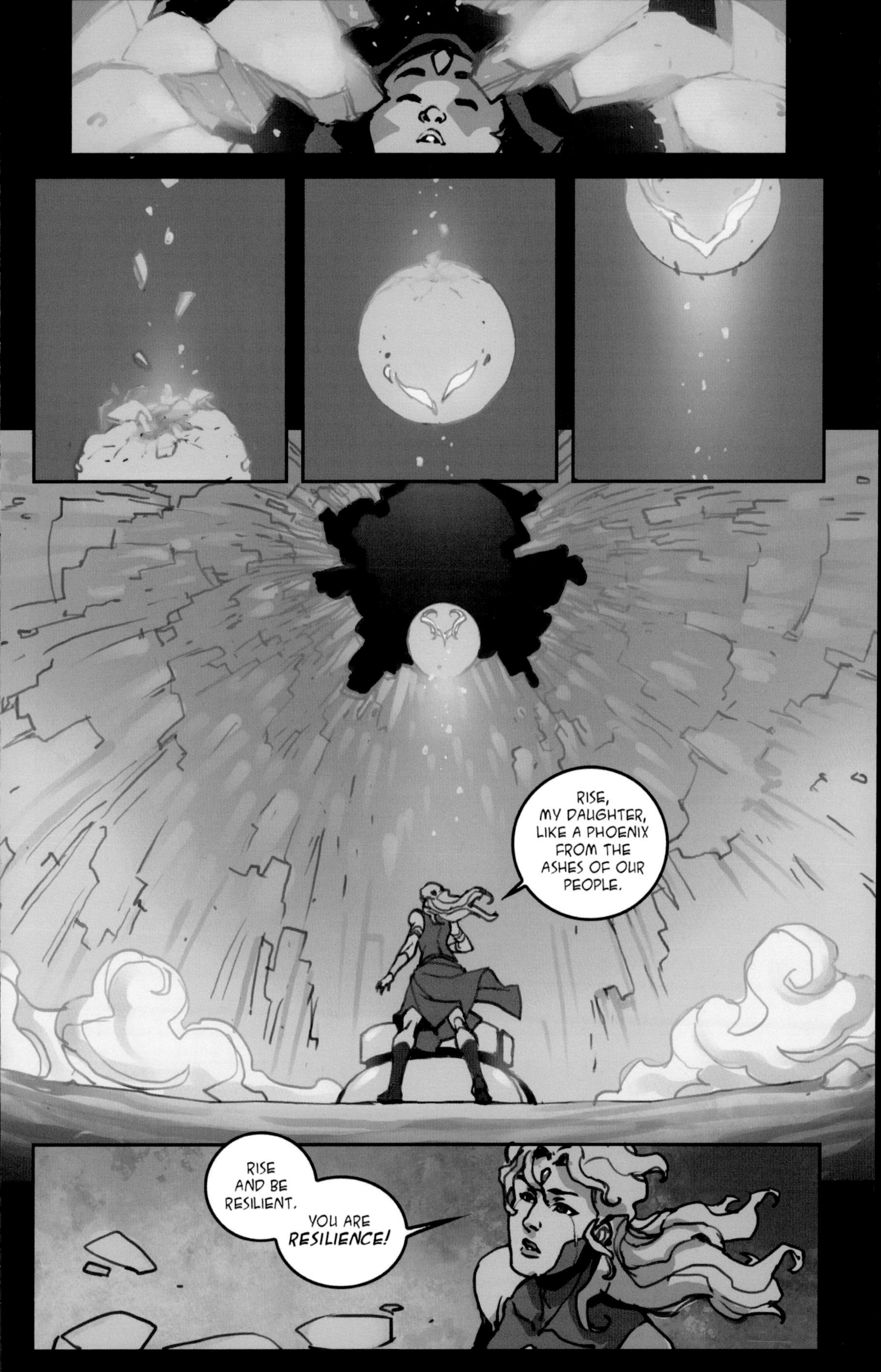
RISE, MY DAUGHTER, LIKE A PHOENIX FROM THE ASHES OF OUR PEOPLE.
RISE AND BE RESILIENT.
YOU ARE RESILIENCE!

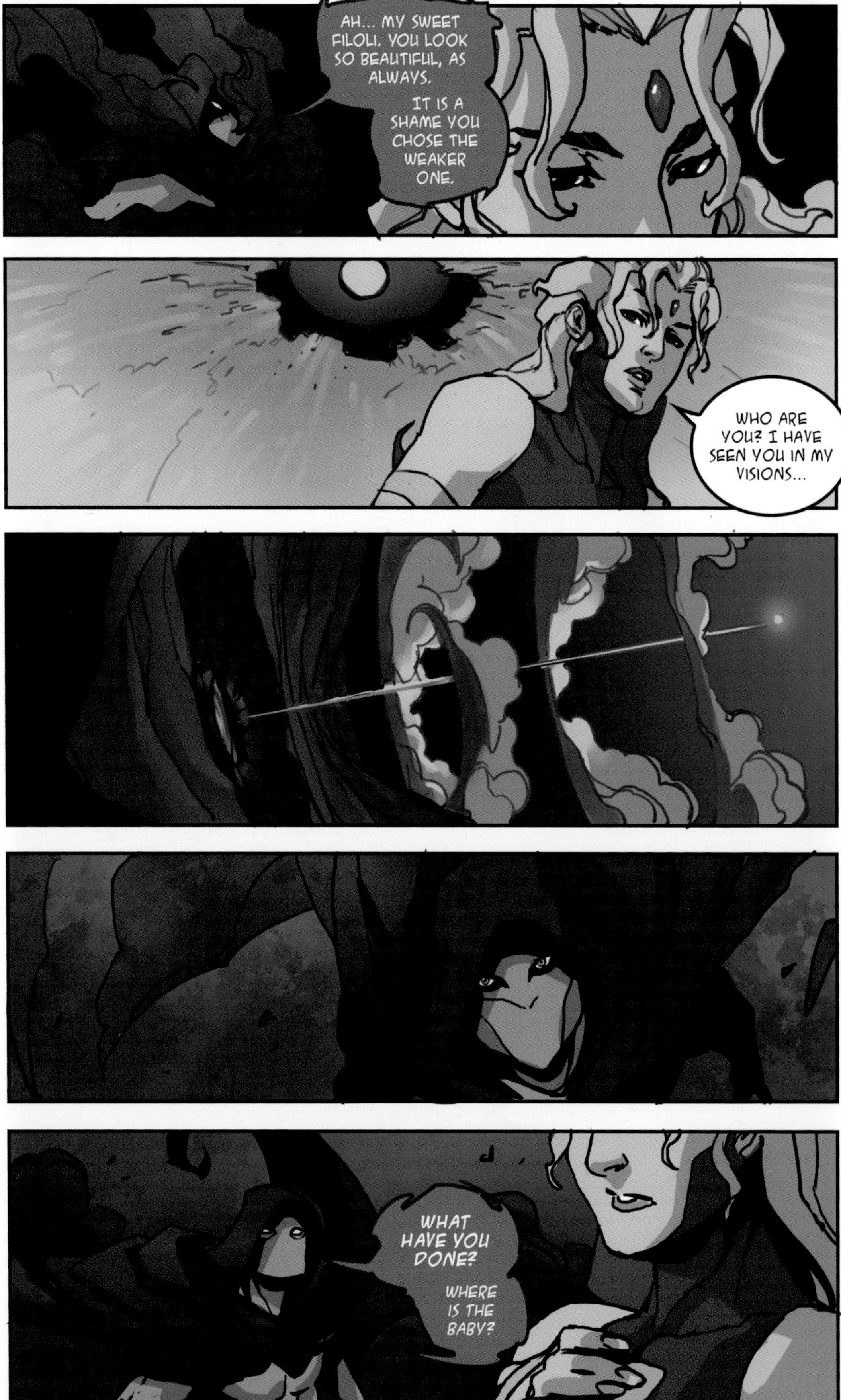
AH... MY SWEET FILOLI. YOU LOOK SO BEAUTIFUL, AS ALWAYS.
IT IS A SHAME YOU CHOSE THE WEAKER ONE.
WHO ARE YOU? I HAVE SEEN YOU IN MY VISIONS...
WHAT HAVE YOU DONE?
WHERE IS THE BABY?

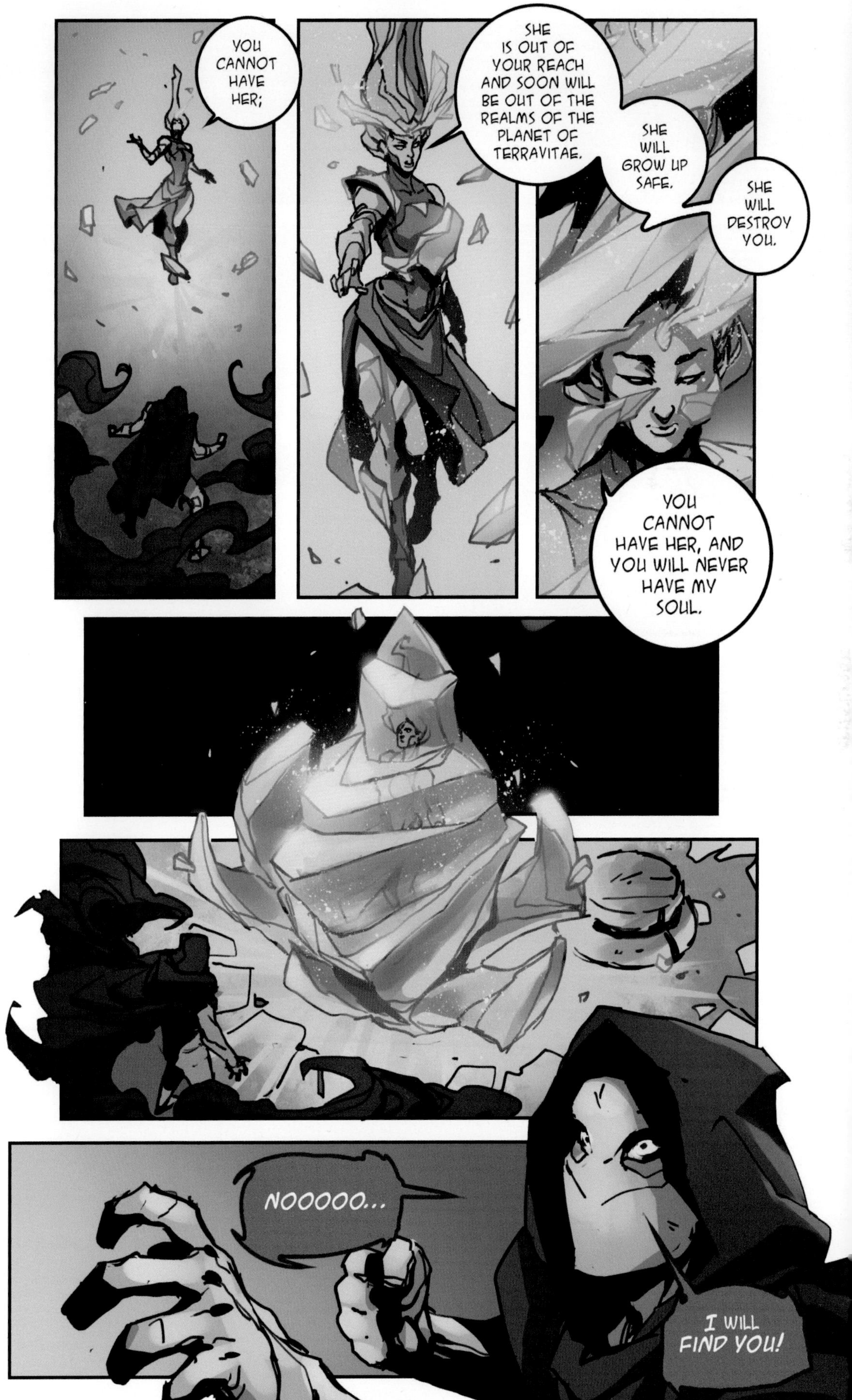
YOU CANNOT HAVE HER;
SHE IS OUT OF YOUR REACH AND SOON WILL BE OUT OF THE REALMS OF THE PLANET OF TERRAVITAE.
SHE WILL GROW UP SAFE.
SHE WILL DESTROY YOU.
YOU CANNOT HAVE HER, AND YOU WILL NEVER HAVE MY SOUL.
NOOOOO...
I WILL FIND YOU!

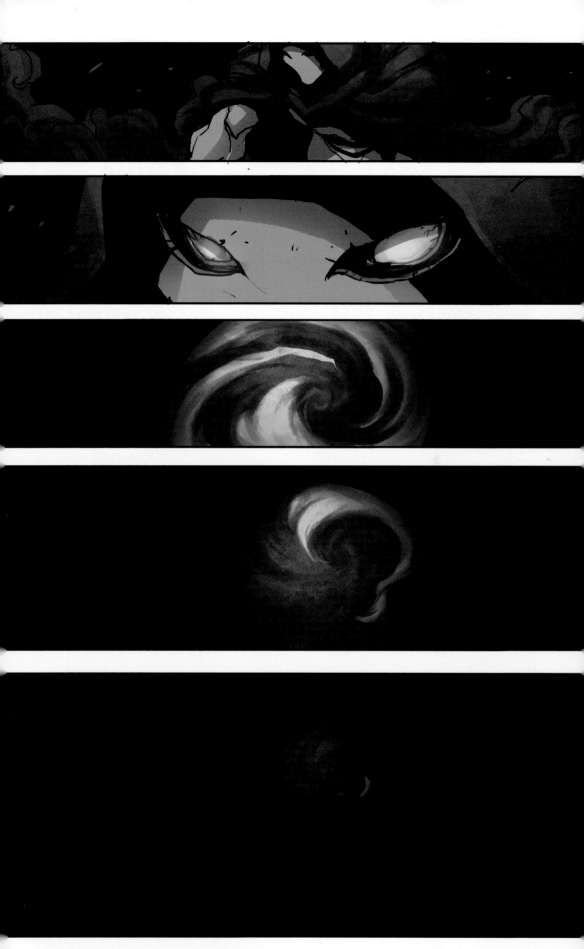

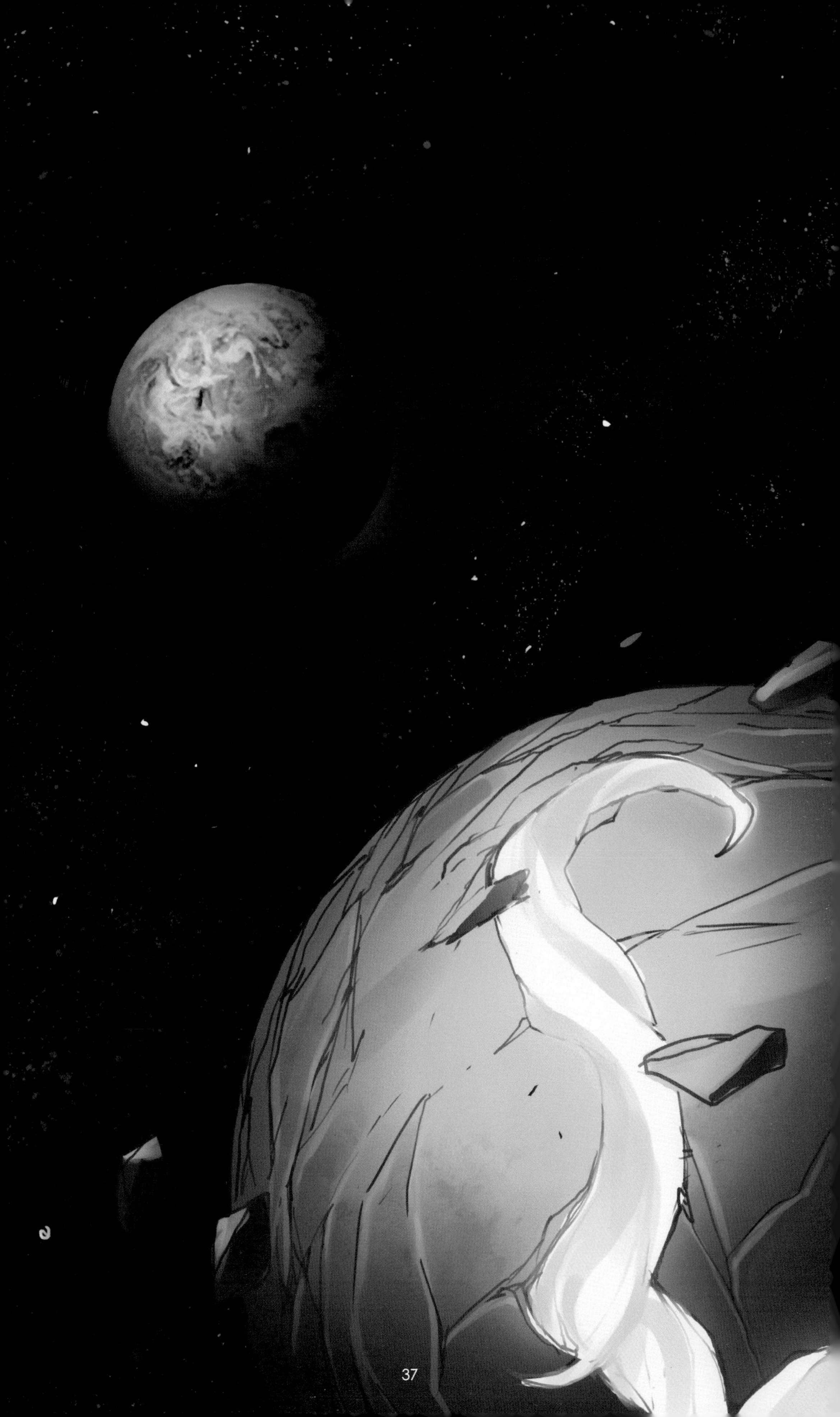

FOLLOW ME

RBRORG.com

ResilienceBirthright

ResilienceBirthright

ResilienceBRite

resiliencebirthright.blog

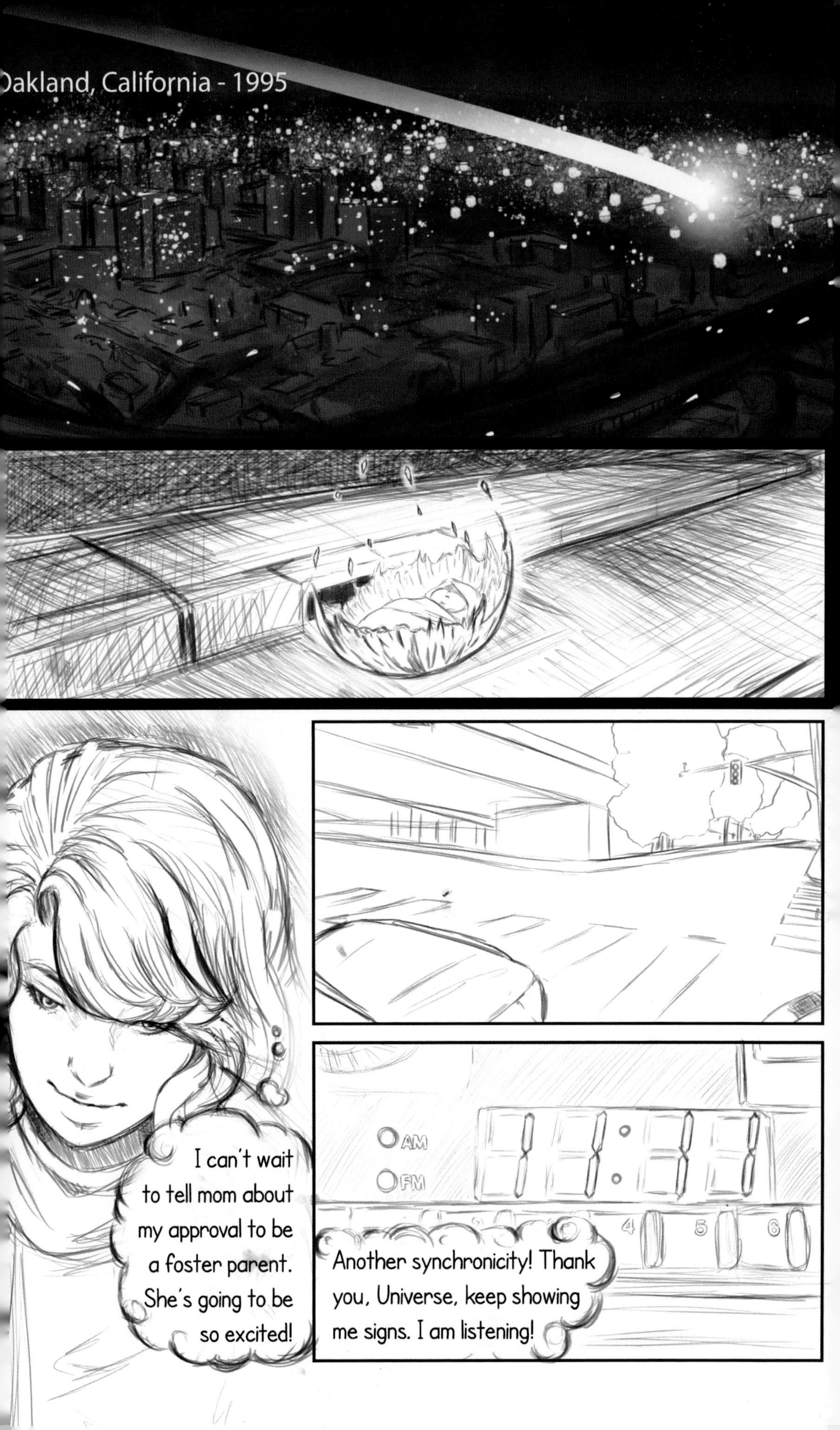
Oakland, California - 1995
AM
FM
4
5
6
I can't wait to tell mom about my approval to be a foster parent. She's going to be so excited!
Another synchronicity! Thank you, Universe, keep showing me signs. I am listening!

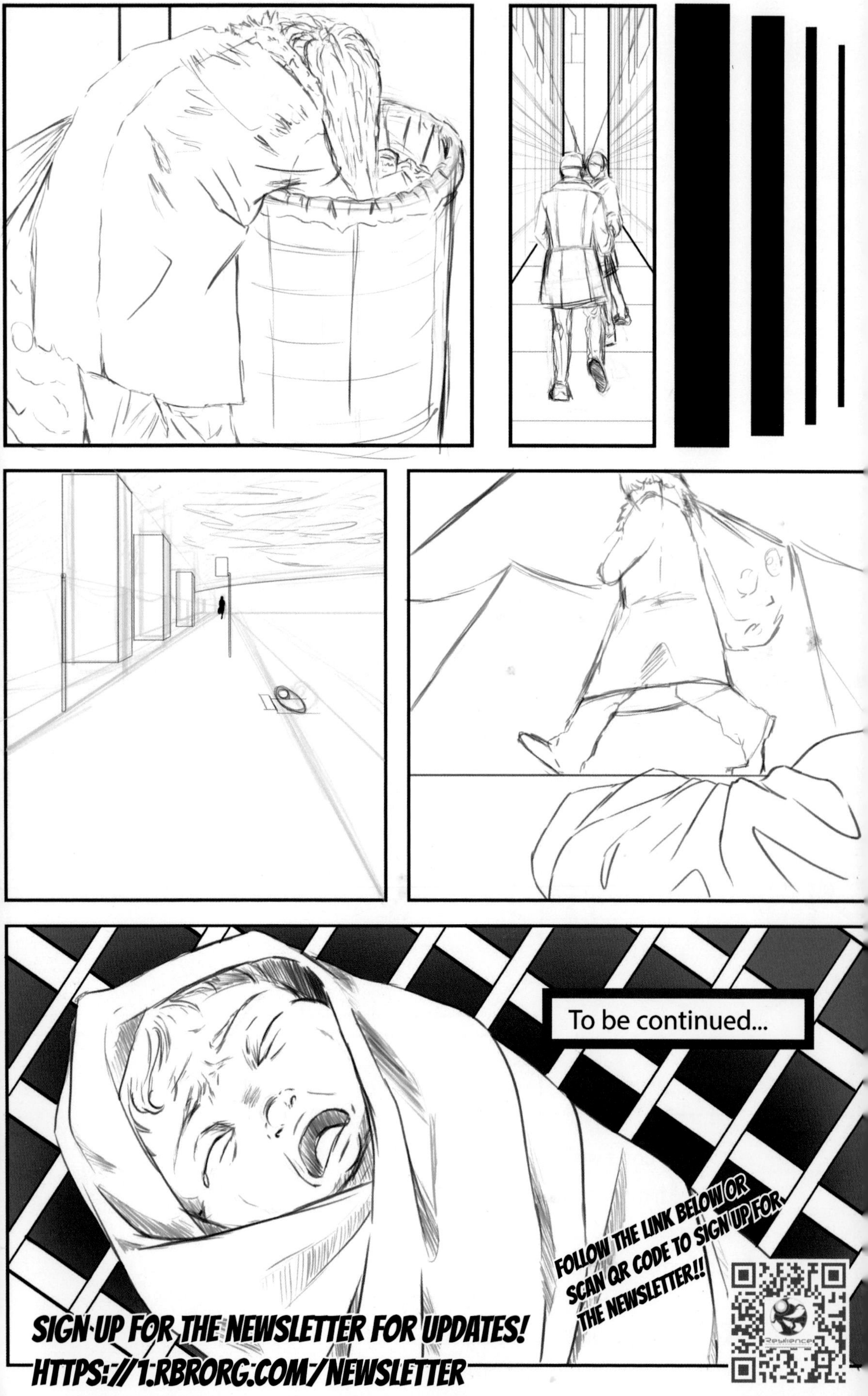
To be continued...
FOLLOW THE LINK BELOW OR SCAN QR CODE TO SIGN UP FOR THE NEWSLETTER!!
SIGN UP FOR THE NEWSLETTER FOR UPDATES!
HTTPS://1.RBRORG.COM/NEWSLETTER

ABOUT: RESILIENCE BIRTHRIGHT SAGA

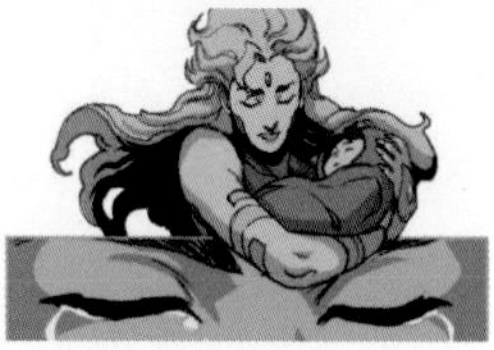

The Resilience Birthright Saga Season One is a thirteen-chapter story about Resilience, an Evolusarian from Planet Terravitae, raised on Earth as an earthling.

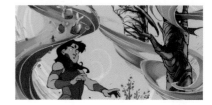

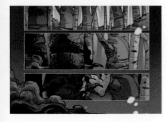

Her destiny is to stop her nemesis, Apophis, from destroying the planet. The Saga reveals Resilience's internal challenges as she breaks through her mental blocks and insecurities to fulfill her destiny and become a hero.

The friends Resilience meets through her journey also have stories of personal truths that shed light on how individual choices and daily actions contribute to the planet for better or worse.

MY DEAR SISTER, CHANGE WILL HAPPEN,
WHAT HAS BEEN SWORN BETWEEN THE FOUR CORNERS WORLDS WILL BE BROKEN,
A BREACH WILL OCCUR, AND THE PALACE OF TERRAVITAE AND ALL LIFE ITSELF WILL BE THREATENED.

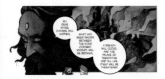

Once she accepts her calling she finds herself thrown into a war between the forces of good and evil as Apophis's army looms closer.

Will she be able to stop Apophis's nefarious plans in time?

IT'S TIME TO AWAKEN THE DARK ARMY.
I WILL TAKE ALL THAT IS MINE.
I WILL LEAVE NO SOUL UNTOUCHED.
29

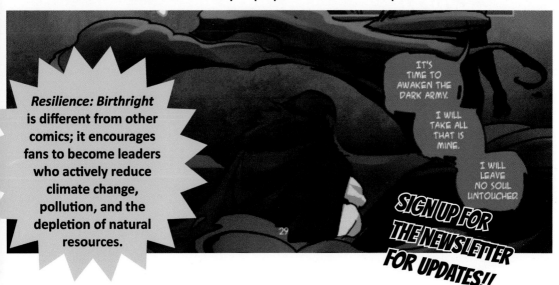

Resilience: Birthright **is different from other comics; it encourages fans to become leaders who actively reduce climate change, pollution, and the depletion of natural resources.**

SIGN UP FOR THE NEWSLETTER FOR UPDATES!!

These stories are based on real heroes who help restore our planet and address actual environmental challenges through fictional storytelling and characters.

SCAN THE QR CODE OR FOLLOW THE LINK BELOW TO SIGN UP FOR THE NEWSLETTER!
HTTPS://1.RBRORG.COM/NEWSLETTER

Resilience

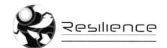

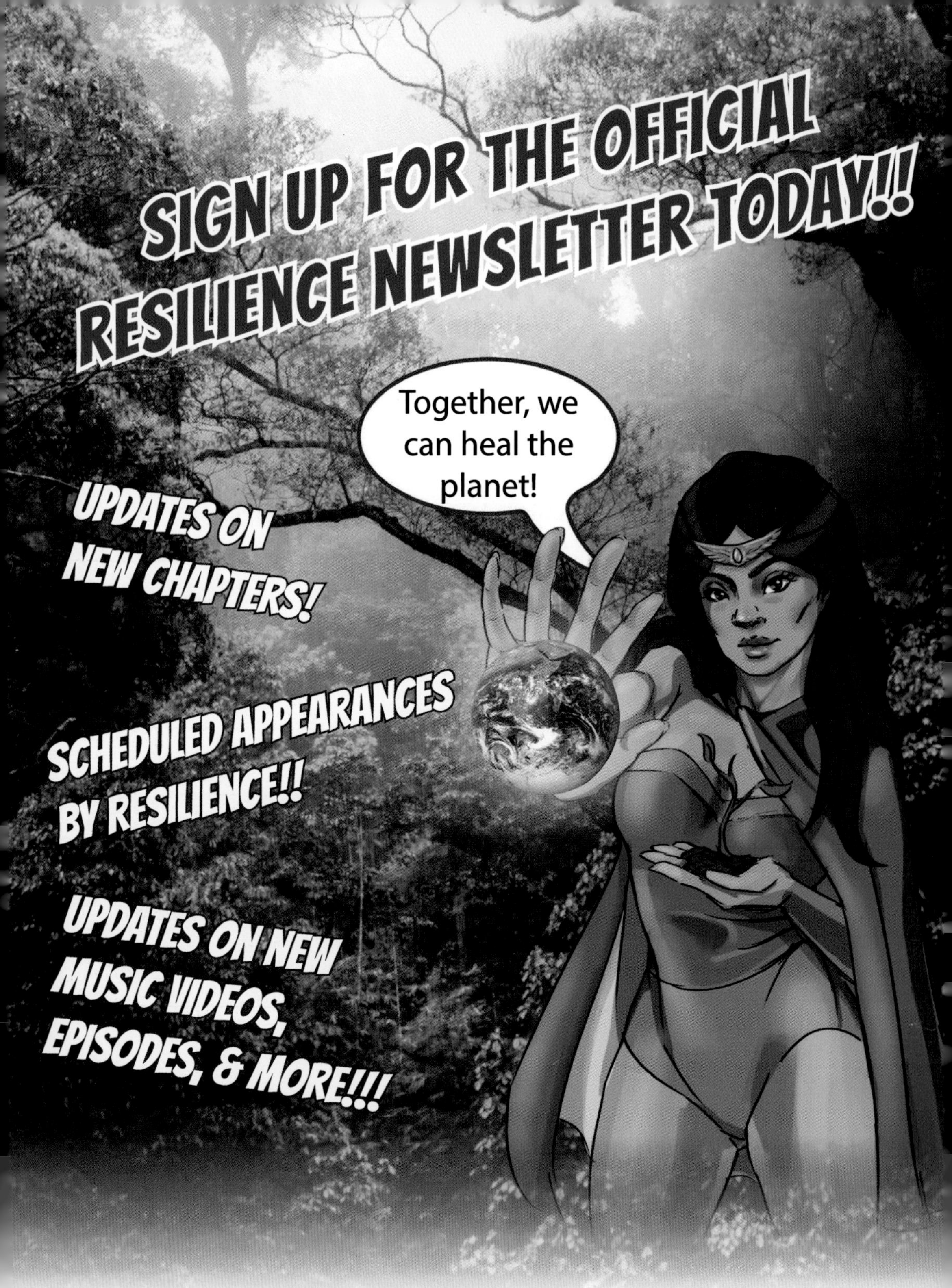
SIGN UP FOR THE OFFICIAL RESILIENCE NEWSLETTER TODAY!!
Together, we can heal the planet!
UPDATES ON NEW CHAPTERS!
SCHEDULED APPEARANCES BY RESILIENCE!!
UPDATES ON NEW MUSIC VIDEOS, EPISODES, & MORE!!!

BE THE FIRST TO KNOW! SCAN THE QR CODE OR FOLLOW THE LINK BELOW TO SIGN UP FOR THE OFFICIAL RESILIENCE NEWSLETTER TODAY!

HTTPS://1.RBRORG.COM/NEWSLETTER

Resilience

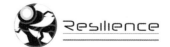

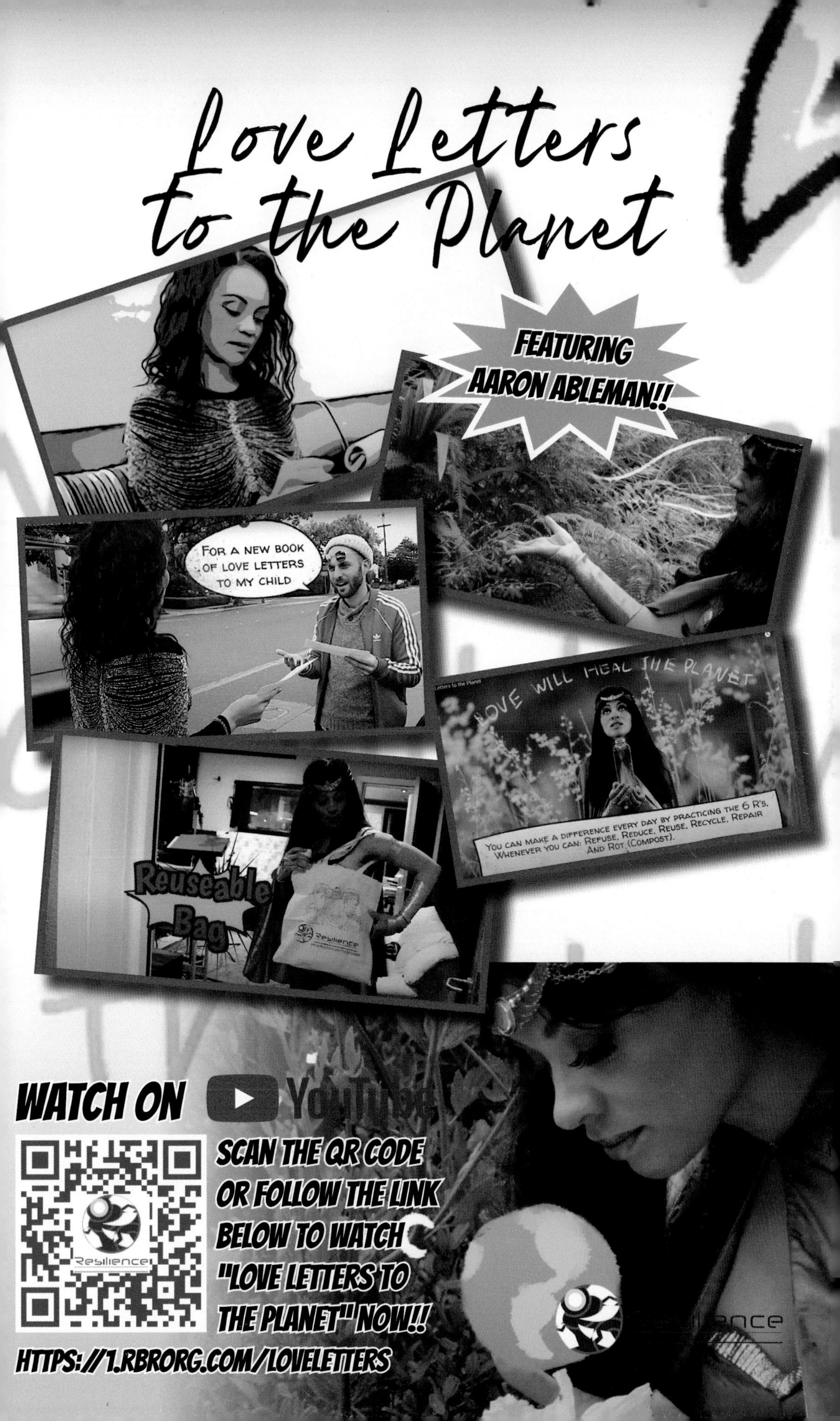
Love Letters to the Planet
FEATURING AARON ABLEMAN!!
FOR A NEW BOOK OF LOVE LETTERS TO MY CHILD
Letters to the Planet
LOVE WILL HEAL THE PLANET
You can make a difference every day by practicing the 6 R's, Whenever you can: Refuse, Reduce, Reuse, Recycle, Repair And Rot (Compost).
Reuseable Bag
Resilience
WATCH ON YouTube
SCAN THE QR CODE OR FOLLOW THE LINK BELOW TO WATCH "LOVE LETTERS TO THE PLANET" NOW!!
HTTPS://1.RBRORG.COM/LOVELETTERS

Love is the Cure

**NEW MUSIC VIDEO!
WATCH NOW!!**

Love is the Cure!

WATCH ON ▶ YouTube

**SCAN THE QR CODE
OR FOLLOW THE LINK
BELOW TO WATCH
"LOVE IS THE CURE"
NOW!!**

HTTPS://1.RBRORG.COM/LOVEISTHECURE

Resilience

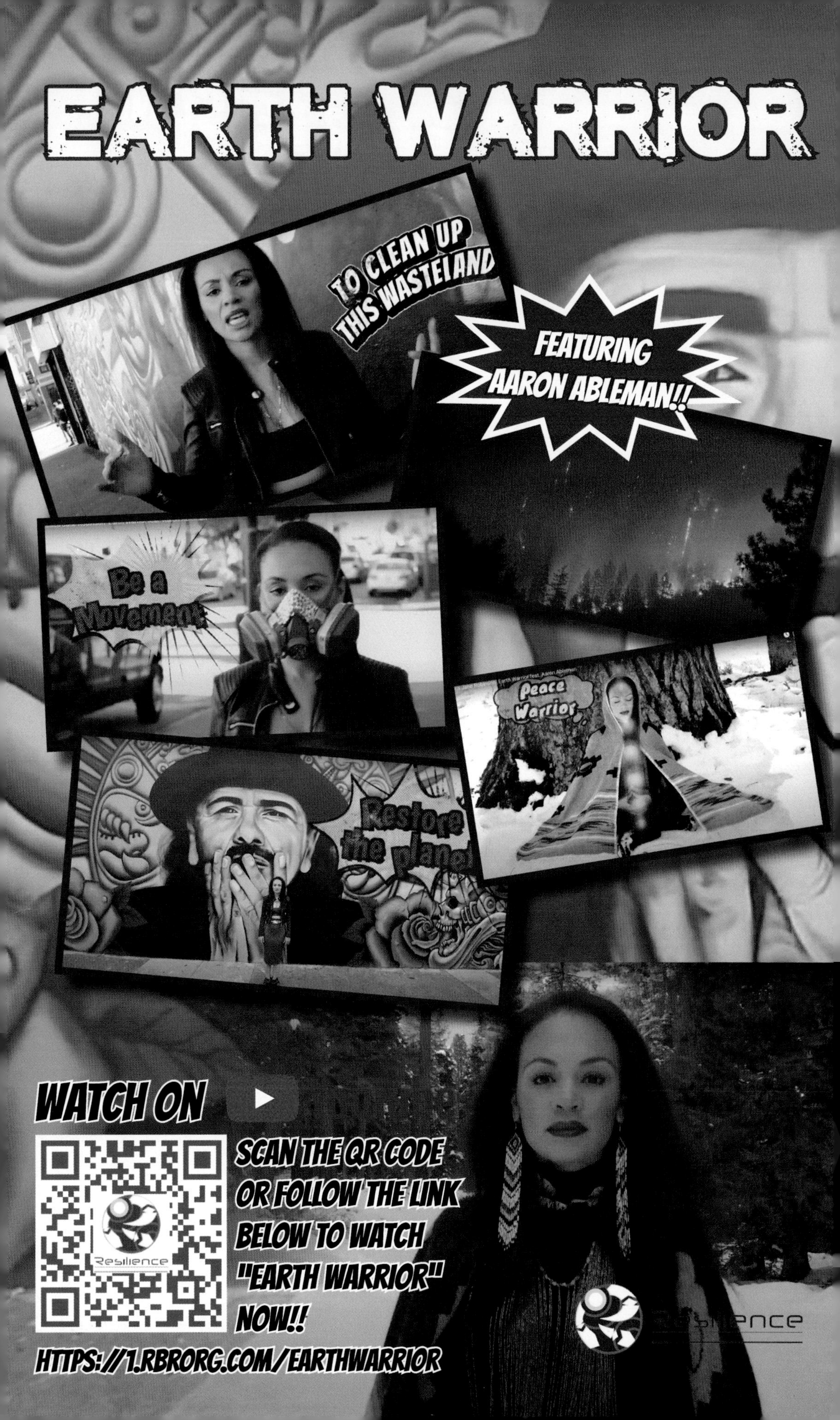

EARTH WARRIOR
TO CLEAN UP THIS WASTELAND
FEATURING AARON ABLEMAN!!
Be a Movement
Peace Warrior
Restore the planet
WATCH ON
SCAN THE QR CODE OR FOLLOW THE LINK BELOW TO WATCH "EARTH WARRIOR" NOW!!
HTTPS://1.RBRORG.COM/EARTHWARRIOR
Resilience
Resilience

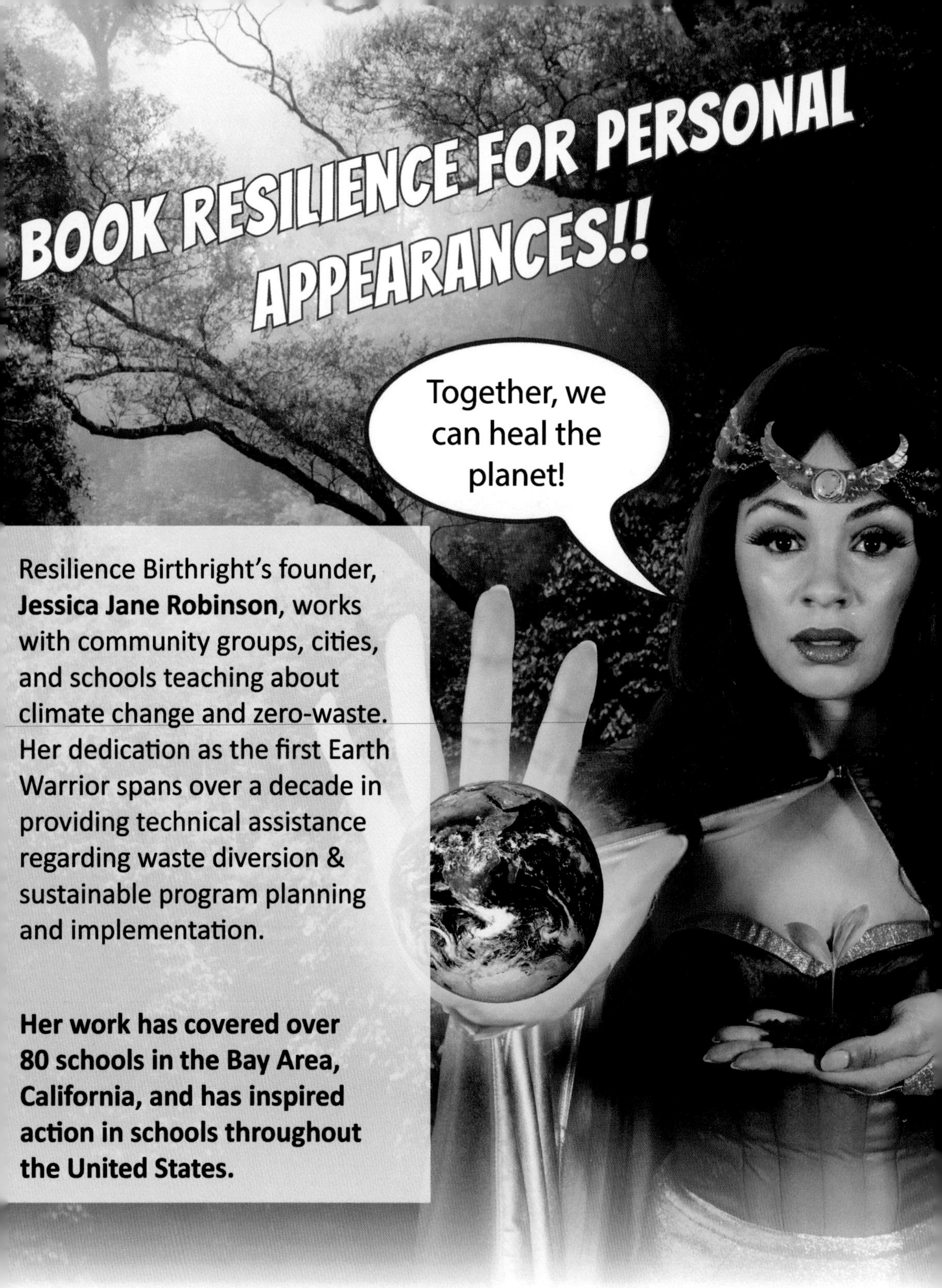
BOOK RESILIENCE FOR PERSONAL APPEARANCES!!
Together, we can heal the planet!

Resilience Birthright's founder, **Jessica Jane Robinson**, works with community groups, cities, and schools teaching about climate change and zero-waste. Her dedication as the first Earth Warrior spans over a decade in providing technical assistance regarding waste diversion & sustainable program planning and implementation.

Her work has covered over 80 schools in the Bay Area, California, and has inspired action in schools throughout the United States.

SCAN THE QR CODE OR FOLLOW THE LINK BELOW TO READ MORE ABOUT RESILIENCE AND BOOK AN APPEARANCE TODAY!

HTTPS://1.RBRORG.COM/BOOKINGFORM

Resilience

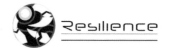

EARTH WARRIOR CARBON CALCULATOR

The Earth Warrior Carbon Calculator is a zero waste 101 tool that helps address climate change and guides people toward 9 of 17 UN Sustainable Development Goals.

This website helps people who are not accustomed to zero waste. Track your daily sustainable actions, such as walking, carpooling, composting, recycling, and reusing. Your activities calculate carbon metric tons avoided from the atmosphere; we then simplify the amount into comparisons, like saving trees or removing cars off the road.

- Waste Reduction 101: Recycle and Compost

- Waste Reduction 201: Reuse and Refuse

- Waste Reduction 301: Refuse Dairy and Meat

- Sustainable Miles Traveled

BE A REAL HERO FOR REAL CHANGE!!
CREATE YOUR FREE ACCOUNT TODAY!

Welcome to **Resilience Birthright**

Earth Warrior Carbon Calculator

View Communities

Register for Free

SCAN THE QR CODE OR FOLLOW THE LINK BELOW TO CREATE YOUR FREE ACCOUNT!

RBRORG.ORG

Resilience

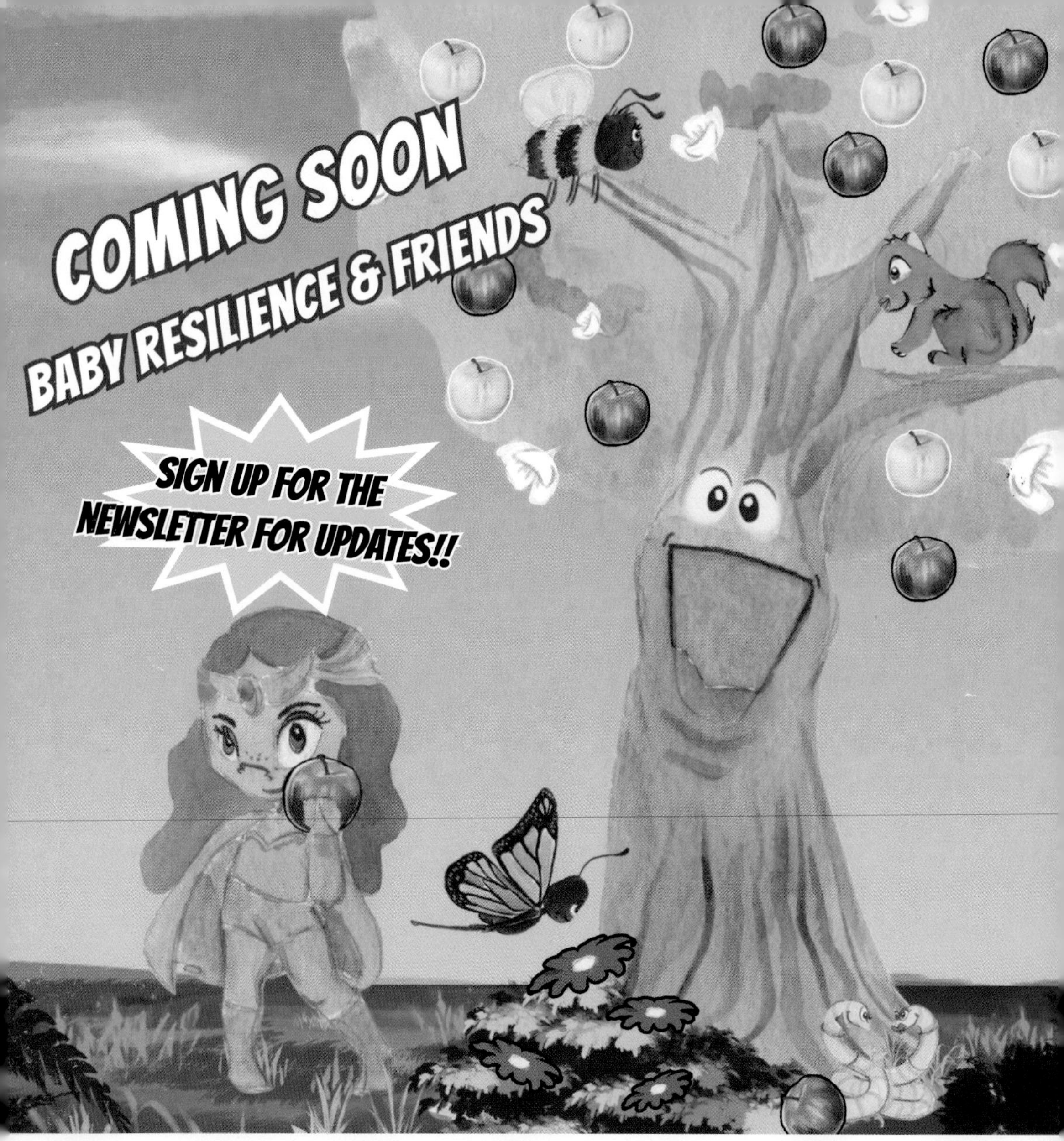
COMING SOON
BABY RESILIENCE & FRIENDS
SIGN UP FOR THE NEWSLETTER FOR UPDATES!!

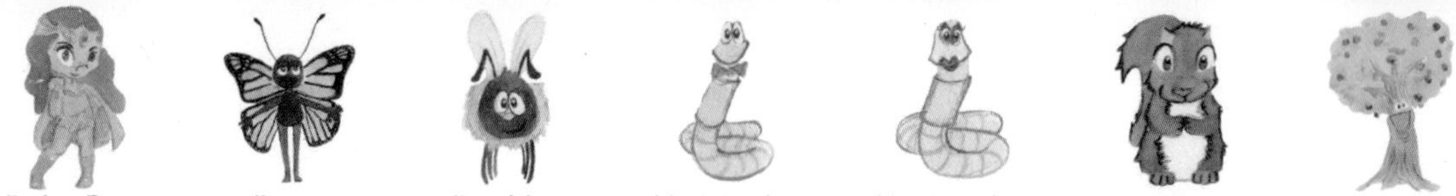

Baby Res | Beau | Bumbles | Mr. Wiggles | Mrs. Wiggles | Sunny | Terry

Each character has their real superhero journey explaining how they do their part to help care for the environment and contribute to making our planet beautiful. "Baby Resilience and Friends" is an educational entertainment book targeting children grades K-2; it includes fun interactive lesson plans that cover Next Generation Science Standards, Common Core Math, and English Language Arts Content Standards.

SCAN THE QR CODE OR FOLLOW THE LINK BELOW TO SIGN UP FOR THE NEWSLETTER!
HTTPS://1.RBRORG.COM/NEWSLETTER

Resilience

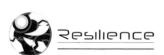